MAX and ME
and the
TIME MACHINE

W9-APH-222

MAX and ME and the
TIME MACHINE

by Gery Greer and Bob Ruddick

A Harper Trophy Book
Harper & Row, Publishers

Library of Congress Catalog Card Number: 87–45284
ISBN 0-06-440222-3 (pbk.)

First Harper Trophy edition, 1988

To Barbara and Scott

and to

Geraldine Greer and C. K. Ruddick

MAX and ME and the TIME MACHINE

1

I guess I'm like everybody else. When I do something that's pretty terrific, I expect to get some credit for it. A little praise, a pat on the back, a bit of wild, thunderous applause—maybe even a chorus of "Bravo! Fantastic! Way to go!"

And that's just what I was expecting when I hauled that huge crate into our clubhouse and told my best friend, Max Zilinski, that it contained a time machine I had picked up at a garage sale down the street. For $2.50.

But Max did not applaud. He snorted.

"Who're you trying to kid, Steve?" he said, barely glancing up from the electronics book he was reading. "There's no such thing as time travel. *Or* time machines."

I wiped the sweat off my forehead with the back of my sleeve and slouched against the crate. "When have I ever lied to you?" I asked, trying to look hurt and sincere at the same time.

"An interesting question," said Max, carefully laying his book aside on the rumpled cot and holding

1

up his fingers to count on. "Now, let me see. I can recall the Rotten Toboggan Affair . . ."

Uh-oh, here we go. Max has all these code names for the various little misunderstandings we've had. The Rotten Toboggan Affair referred to that day last winter when I talked him into going down Quarter-Mile Hill on a beat-up old toboggan. "You're crazy," Max had said. "This hill is too steep and this toboggan is a mess. Look at it. It's even rotting out underneath."

It took a lot of doing, but I finally convinced him that the toboggan was as good as new and as sound as a rock. A couple of minutes later, as we were tearing down the hill at about eighty miles an hour, the toboggan began to come apart. Little pieces began breaking off, and we lost control, hit a tree stump, somersaulted through the air, and smashed into a snowbank. Max remembers things like that.

". . . and the Taste-Tempting Tip . . ."

Was it my fault that liver-and-kidney-flavored Puppy Chewies taste worse, not better, than they look?

". . . and let's not forget Operation Lousy Letter!"

See what happens when you try to help a friend? I mean, could I have known that Max, who is always trying to work up the nerve to talk to Dawn Sharington, would get upset when I broke the ice by writing her a love letter and signing his name to it?

"Okay, okay," I said, holding up my hands in surrender. "Let's not quibble over a few minor mistakes. After all, what do you care if Dawn knows you think she's the best-looking girl west of the Mississippi?"

Max made a choking sound.

"Besides, you should thank me. You wanted

Dawn to notice you, and now she does. Whenever she sees you, she starts giggling like crazy."

"Agggggggh," groaned Max, clutching his head with both hands.

"Look, Max," I said cheerfully, "forget about the letter. We've got something a lot more important to deal with. I mean, haven't we been wondering for the last two weeks what we were going to do all summer? Well, now we've got the answer."

I patted the time-machine crate meaningfully and read the black lettering stamped on the side: MAINLY, ONE GENUINE, COMPLETELY AUTOMATED, EASILY ASSEMBLED, ONE-OF-A-KIND TIME MACHINE! FULLY GUARANTEED!

"Sure, sure," grumbled Max. "And you got it at a garage sale for two fifty. You don't expect me to believe that, do you?"

"If you'll just listen a minute," I said, "I can explain the whole thing. Okay?"

Max grunted, but he was still suffering over Dawn. This sales pitch was going to have to be good.

"Okay. You know Mr. Cooper, right? The man who lives just around the corner in that great big old house? Well, he found this crate in his attic last night, and he's sure it was left there by the famous Professor Flybender."

Max's logical mind slowly clicked into gear. "Oh, yeah? If this professor guy is so famous, how come I've lived here in Flat Rock for five years and never heard of him? And why would he leave things in Mr. Cooper's attic?"

"Good points. I asked Mr. Cooper the same

things. It turns out that Flybender used to live there and was some sort of crazy inventor. You know, setting off explosions in his basement and racing around on his roof during thunderstorms. About eight years ago, he announced that he was off to find the lost continent of Atlantis, and nobody has seen him since. Eventually, the house was sold to pay off the professor's debts, and Mr. Cooper bought it."

"Okay, Sherlock, then why didn't Mr. Cooper find this marvelous invention before now?" Max smugly pushed his glasses back up on his nose.

"Because, Watson, there was so much junk in the attic when Mr. Cooper bought the house he never had time to go through it all. But this morning he was looking for stuff to put on sale, and that's when he spotted the crate. He dragged it down and put it out with a bunch of chipped dishes and old clothes."

"I still say you've been had," Max insisted stubbornly. "If Mr. Cooper actually believed this was a time machine, do you really think he would have sold it to you?"

"Of course not," I scoffed. I was ready for that one, too. "But just because Mr. Cooper is too shortsighted to recognize a great discovery like this doesn't mean we have to be, too. After all, you're the one who's always telling me that scientific geniuses are misunderstood in their own times."

Max seemed impressed with this argument, since it was one of his own. Nibbling his thumbnail thoughtfully, he got up and began to circle the crate slowly.

"Well, just for the sake of argument," he said, "let's *suppose* this Professor Flybender really was a brilliant inventor, and *suppose* he really did build this thing, and *suppose* he really did leave it in Mr. Cooper's attic . . ."

Max's voice trailed off as he mulled over his supposes.

Max is like that. He *thinks* about everything, weighing all the angles, considering all the options. Maybe it comes from being a compulsive reader. I mean, Max goes for books like a hungry piranha goes for toes, which means he knows *something* about almost everything. It also means his brain works overtime. I call him Motor-Mind.

As for me, I prefer action. It saves time. I can eat two ice-cream cones in the time it takes Max to consider the relative merits of vanilla versus peanut-pumpkin swirl.

And I could see it was time to act. I thumped the crate loudly with the flat of my hand—THUMP.

"Max, my boy, this is Opportunity Knocking." THUMP, THUMP. "Think of it—a *time machine*! A hot rod into history! Why, with this baby we could go anywhere we want—to any *time* we want. Just consider the possibilities!"

THUMP! "We could travel back three thousand years to ancient Egypt and catch the grave robbers as they jimmy their way into King Tut's tomb!"

Max's eyes glazed slightly as he considered that possibility.

THUMP! "We could ride with Attila the Hun and his mighty hordes as they terrorize the Roman Empire!"

"Yeah," whispered Max in an awed voice. "And if

we stopped off in the seventeenth century, I could get Shakespeare's autograph!"

He was hooked. Of course, I had no intention of chasing around through time trying to get some guy's autograph, but we could iron out that detail later.

I hopped up onto a stool. "We could drop in on the nineteenth century and solve the Jack the Ripper murders!"

"Wow!" said Max, joining in. "And attend the opening night of Beethoven's Fifth Symphony!"

I jabbed my finger at the ceiling and cried, "Babe Ruth, Billy the Kid, Blackbeard the Pirate!"

"Aristotle, Galileo, Einstein!" Max shouted.

I made a flying leap onto the table, threw back my head, and yelled, "The Gunfight at the O.K. Corral!"

Max was overcome. He snapped to attention and saluted up at me. "Say no more, chief," he said, his face glowing with enthusiasm. "Just tell me what you want me to do."

I jumped down and held out my hand. "Fork over two dollars," I said. "I was a little short of the asking price, and Mr. Cooper said he'd take the time machine back if I didn't come up with the rest of the money before eleven o'clock."

2

Putting the time machine together was a cinch. We just followed the step-by-step instructions in the professor's booklet on ASSEMBLING FLYBENDER'S FANTASTIC, FULLY GUARANTEED TIME MACHINE. Nobody bothered us either, which is one of the big advantages of having a clubhouse of our own. We'd built it ourselves out in my backyard, where it's almost completely hidden by trees. Even my nosy little sister usually leaves us alone.

By one o'clock, the time machine was finished. As we shook hands and stood back to admire our work, the weird seven-foot-tall contraption seemed to be staring down at us.

"We may have just assembled Flybender's Fantastic Hunk of Junk," commented Max, eyeing the machine doubtfully. "Does this thing look like a time machine to you?"

"You bet," I lied. "And what a beaut."

Actually, Max had a point. It did look sort of like a hunk of junk. In fact, with all the confusion of dials and meters and switches and colored lights, and that ridiculously tiny map of the world pinned under glass, and that enormous ON-OFF lever jutting out from the side, the machine could have been anything. Mostly, it looked like a giant jelly-bean dispenser from outer space.

As for the inner workings, they were a complete mystery, because most of the work we'd done was limited to screwing knobs and glass plates and other loose parts onto the outer surface of the machine. Like, for instance, the overgrown fan that, following the professor's instructions, we had bolted on top. I had the uneasy feeling that if we turned that fan on, it would turn the clubhouse inside out.

All in all, it was hard to believe Flybender's machine could transport anybody anywhere—especially through time. But I wasn't going to waste time worrying about it. I believe in positive thinking.

While I cleaned up, Max fine tuned the controls, checking the instruction manual to see that the meters were calibrated, the switches were in the correct positions, and all buttons had been pushed in the proper sequence.

I guess you'd say that next to reading, Max's favorite pastime is tinkering with mechanical gadgets. He even put together a pretty impressive robot once, named Big Ed. Last summer we smuggled it up to Camp Wongahana and into a closet in our group's cabin. Then, when all the lights were out, and right in the middle of one of Sid Berman's hair-raising ghost stories, Max pushed a button on his hand-held, remote-control unit, and Big Ed came slamming out of the closet door. His face glowed like a ghoul's, and he made a horrible gurgling noise. Of course, if Sid hadn't been telling ghost stories at the time, everybody probably wouldn't have panicked the way they did, and our counselor wouldn't have led that stampede out of the cabin, screaming, "It's the Un-dead! It's the Un-dead!"

So Max couldn't take *all* the credit for how he and I and Big Ed had the whole cabin to ourselves for the next couple of hours.

Still, he does have a way with machines.

"That's it," said Max, snapping the manual shut. "According to the professor, all we have to do now is select a time and place we want to visit. When our time is up, we'll be automatically returned to the present. And no matter how long we're gone, no time will have passed here, so no one will even know we've been away."

"You mean we'll come back exactly when we left?" I asked.

"That's what the manual says," said Max.

"Great!" I said, pacing the floor with excitement. "And of course since I found the time machine, I get to choose where we go on our first trip. And I choose the Middle Ages."

"The Middle Ages?" said Max, with a puzzled frown. "What's so great about the Middle Ages?"

I slapped my forehead in disgust. "Have you been asleep for the last thirteen years, or what? Haven't you ever heard of knights in shining armor? Haven't you heard of castles and dungeons and damsels in distress? Wouldn't you like a little Action, Adventure, and Excitement?"

"No," said Max.

"I can see it now," I continued, striking a gallant pose. "There we'd be, galloping over the green hills and through the dark forests, rescuing fair maidens who are in danger up to their armpits."

Max snorted. "Everyone knows that all that stuff about rescuing damsels in distress is just a bunch of bunk."

"Oh, yeah? I don't suppose you've ever thought about how it'd be to rescue Dawn Sharington from distress."

Max blushed. "Well," he grumbled, quickly changing the topic, "if we're going to the Middle Ages, we're going to have to nail down the exact date. How does 1250 A.D. sound? That would put us right in the middle of the best century of the whole Middle Ages."

"Whatever you say," I agreed. "You're the history expert."

Max bent toward the control panel of the time machine, squinting. I peered over his shoulder. All the controls were preset except for the three in the center of the panel, outlined with a ring of colored lights. The first was marked "Dial-a-Date." By turning the knobs under the window, you could dial any date you wanted. Max carefully dialed A.D. 1250.

The second control, "Pick-a-Place," had a tiny world map under glass. Max fiddled with the knobs and found that they moved a red dot across the face of the map, marking the place you wanted to be transported to.

"Might as well make it jolly old England," he said, jockeying the red dot into position.

I couldn't believe it—a trip to medieval England!

My skin prickled, and I began to beat out a drum roll on the table.

"As for our 'Length-of-Stay,' " continued Max briskly as he examined the third control, "since this is a trial run, I say we drop in for about three hours."

"*Three hours*!" The drums stopped in midroll. "*Three hours*! What can we do in three measly little hours?"

"We can stay out of trouble, that's what." Max squared his shoulders and crossed his arms over his chest. "Take it or leave it. I'm crazy enough just letting you talk me into trying this thing in the first place."

He meant it.

"You win," I sighed.

With a satisfied nod, Max turned to adjust the "Length-of-Stay" controls. He set the numbers knobs to read "003" and then spun the units knob past "Years" and "Days" to lock in on "Hours." Three hours. Big deal. Baseball games can last longer than that.

I was disappointed, and I guess that's why I did it. I know I shouldn't have, but when Max took his glasses off to polish them on his shirt tail, I reached over and moved the last numbers knob forward five notches. What could it hurt if we were in the Middle Ages for eight hours instead of three?

To cover myself, I kept an eye on Max and observed loudly, "Do you realize what this means? We're actually going to travel through time! You and me. Steve Brandon and Maximilian Zilinski."

"Yeah." Max's voice wavered, as if he weren't too sure he really liked the idea. "Maybe we should gather up some supplies or sandwiches or something and go tomorrow morning. What do you think?"

I hate waiting. Besides, waiting might give Max time to change his mind.

"There's no time like the present," I said.

"Then why are we going to the Middle Ages?" said Max dryly.

He put his glasses back on and started for the door. "Anyway," he added, "why don't we go over to my house and have something to eat? My mother can make us one of her famous avocado-and-chili sandwiches, and we can talk the whole thing over."

I figured it was now or never.

Almost without thinking, I reached out, grasped the huge ON-OFF lever, and by throwing my full weight against it, pulled it down to "ON." Max spun around, but there was nothing he could do. He was clear across the room, with his hand on the doorknob and one foot out the door. I barely had time to glimpse his startled expression before Professor Flybender's Fully Guaranteed Time Machine sprang to life.

3

Lights flashed, gauges gyrated, steam spewed out of loose joints with the force of a fire hose turned on full blast.

Flybender's machine was working, all right.

Then, from deep inside, came a weird, wild, wailing sound. It was low like a moan but rose steadily until it reached an eerie high pitch. And at that moment the giant fan on top of the machine began to spin, ghostly slow at first, but gaining speed . . . faster . . . faster . . .

The clubhouse began to vibrate . . . faster. . . . I was thrown up hard against the shaking walls . . . faster. . . . Max began to look fuzzy around the edges . . . faster. . . . Now he was a blur . . . faster. . . .

"*Max!*" I shouted. And was immediately plunged into darkness.

The wind whistled by in furious whirlwinds, howling around my head and pulling at my hair. I felt as if I were on a vibrating conveyor belt, out of control and hurtling through a long ink-black tunnel.

A panicky feeling welled up inside me. I pushed it

down and tried to call out to Max, but the wind caught his name and swept it away.

Where was Max? Why was this taking so long? Why weren't we in the Middle Ages? Why—

Without warning, the vibrating stopped, and I fell several feet, landing with a heavy thud.

It was all over, but where was I? There were no lights, no sounds.

Blinking into the blackness, I tried to look around, but for some reason I couldn't move my neck. I tried to stand up but discovered that I couldn't move my legs. I tried a dog-paddle, but it was no go. *I was pinned*.

Now what? I wondered grimly.

Suddenly, I was startled by a strange, clinky-jingling noise and the uncomfortable feeling that I was turning, like a chicken on a barbecue spit, slowl-l-l-l-ly in space.

A narrow slit of light appeared in front of my eyes.

Then, into that slit of light popped a face—round, eager, about sixteen years old, with brown bobbed hair. He examined me with concern for a few moments before asking anxiously, "Art thou all right, Sir Robert?"

Before I could answer, the round-faced stranger pulled me to a sitting position and lifted a massive, flat-topped helmet off my head. I gaped down at myself in amazement.

No wonder I made a clinking noise whenever I moved. My T-shirt, jeans, and tennis shoes were gone. In their place was a long chain-mail shirt that covered me from head to knee, and underneath that, a pair of chain-mail tights. Over the armor, I was sporting a sleeveless, emerald-green tunic with a coat of arms embroidered in gold across my chest. And from my belt hung a long sword in a gold scabbard.

But even more amazing, I was wearing *someone else's body*! Someone tall and broad-shouldered, with plenty of well-developed muscles.

Not bad, I thought to myself, as I flexed my arm and felt the muscles ripple.

"Art thou all right, Sir Robert?" repeated the stranger. He was wearing a simple brown tunic over green tights, and soft leather boots with pointed toes.

"I sure art," I said cheerfully. As I spoke, I noticed that even my voice was different. It was deeper than my own, and stronger too. "But if you don't mind my asking, who art you?"

"Why, I am Niles, Sir Robert. Thy squire. Dost thou not know me?" He shook his head and looked worried. "Thou hast taken a nasty tumble off thy horse, and methinks it hath rattled thy wits."

He was wrong there. My wits were in tip-top condition. In fact, you might say that my wits were doing handsprings for joy as I realized several things:

- Flybender's machine had worked after all, and I was in the Middle Ages as planned.
- I had been transported into the body of a Sir Robert, a knight, and this guy, Niles, was his squire.
- As I entered Sir Robert's body, I must have gotten dizzy and fallen off my horse, which explained why Niles thought my wits were rattled, and why I had arrived with my nose in the dirt.

Then it hit me. If I came back in someone else's body, Max could be here, too, and I'd never recognize him. I began to look around with serious interest.

I was on a grassy field, surrounded by a makeshift camp of large, brightly colored tents, each decorated with flags and pennants that fluttered in the breeze. Looming a short distance to the right were the gray stone walls and turrets of a medieval castle. And by my side stood a sleek white horse draped with yards and yards of green cloth trimmed in gold.

Here and there men and boys scurried, all dressed like Niles in tunics and tights. Max could be anywhere, even miles from here.

I realized that if I were ever going to find him, I'd need a lot more information. And as Niles helped me to my feet, I thought of a plan to get it.

I shook my head as if I were still dazed. "Niles," I said, hoping I looked lost and confused, "I can't seem to get my bearings. I'm afraid that falling off my horse has made me lose my memory. Maybe if you'd tell me where we are and what we're doing here, it will all come back to me."

It worked. Niles looked up at me anxiously, with loyal devotion written all over his face. "Why, Sir Robert, we are at the Great Hampshire Tournament, where we have camped these past three days in thy tent." He gestured to the yellow-gold tent with green banners that stood behind us. "We came at the invitation of Richard Lorraine, Earl of Hampshire, who heard tales of thy great strength and skill at jousting and would try thee against his own champion. 'Tis the last day of the tourney, and thou art undefeated as usual, sire. Eighteen knights have fallen already before thy lance. There remaineth only the joust with Sir Bevis, a minor feat for someone with thy mighty talents."

I nodded cautiously. "I see. And just when is this minor jousting match supposed to take place?"

"In but a few moments, Sir Robert," he said, busily dusting off my tunic and straightening my belt. "Then the tourney will be over, and thou wilt be the champion. The people await this last joust most eagerly."

"Hmmmm. And you think I can handle Sir Bevis, do you?"

Niles laughed merrily. "Oh, Sir Robert, thou art jesting, of course. 'Twill be a sad day for English knighthood when thou, the Green Falcon, canst not best the likes of Sir Bevis."

Bingo! Jackpot! Things were looking good. Not only was I in the Middle Ages, but I was in the body of a famous knight and was actually going to be in a jousting match on the field of honor! And it was my kind of contest—me against some harmless, lily-livered, mealy-mouthed twerp.

The only problem was that it all sounded a bit beneath my talents. Why then, I wondered, were the people so eager to see this particular match? I decided to fish for a few details.

"Tell me, Niles," I said, cracking my knuckles and flexing my muscles, "who is this Bevis turkey anyway?"

"Why, Sir Bevis Thorkell," replied Niles cheerfully, "the Earl's champion and a knight known throughout all England as the Hampshire Mauler."

"The Hampshire *Mauler*?" I didn't like the sound of that.

"Aye, Sir Robert, and a black-hearted varlet he is. Canst thou truly remember nothing? Dost thou not recall his vow to smash thy skull and feed thy guts to the castle dogs, the saucy fellow?"

Saucy fellow? This was his idea of a saucy fellow? Something began to tell me I might not be cut out for the field of honor after all.

Niles continued gleefully. "Ho, ho! But I did put Sir Bevis in his place. Not two hours ago I met the knave within the castle walls. 'Is thy master ready to meet his doom?' he did ask me. 'Best thou lookest to thine own health,' I replied. 'Sir Robert will this very afternoon whack thee from thy horse, pommel and pound thee, and smite thee to smithereens.' "

"Gee," I said, laughing nervously. "I hope he didn't take that the wrong way."

Niles nodded happily. "That blow to thy head hath not robbed thee of thy sense of humor, Sir Robert." He chuckled contentedly to himself.

I found myself wondering if Sir Bevis and I could talk this thing over. I mean, I didn't want to be a spoilsport or anything, but let's face it, I don't perform well under pressure.

"Niles," I said, looking for an out, "give it to me straight. What has Sir Bevis got against me?"

" 'Tis no secret, sire. Sir Bevis is sore jealous that thou art a knight and are but eighteen years of age. He himself was not knighted until his twenty-first year, as is the common custom. And 'tis well known that the Earl hath taken a liking to thee during the tournament.

Mayhap Sir Bevis feareth that thou wilt replace him as the Earl's champion."

Niles blushed slightly. "And, of course, there is the matter of Lady Elizabeth."

"Oh?" I asked suspiciously. "What matter would that be?"

Niles's blush deepened and he looked away, embarrassed. "Ah, well, since thou hast lost thy memory, Sir Robert, I suppose I must admit that even I have noticed the glances that have passed between thyself and the Earl's fair daughter. And since Sir Bevis hopeth to make the Lady his wife, this hath only angered him the more."

"Okay," I said, shifting my weight uneasily. "Let me get this straight. Sir Bevis is a little upset because he thinks I'm trying to steal his reputation, his job, and his girl. Right?"

"Aye. And thou art just the man to do it."

"But—"

Suddenly, there was a loud blast of trumpets from somewhere nearby.

"Make haste, sire!" gasped Niles. " 'Tis time!"

Before I could say another word, he clapped the iron helmet back onto my head. A page ran out of a nearby tent, carrying some portable stairs which he plunked down next to the white stallion. I was still confused and stunned as Niles hustled me up the stairs and onto the horse, thrusting a shield into my left hand and a ten-foot-long lance into my right.

With a hearty "Go to, Sir Robert!" he slapped the horse's backside, and off we trotted in the direction of the trumpets.

"Where is Max now that I need him?" I groaned.

"Right here," said a deep voice from under me. "And you have my full support!"

It was Max! He was my horse!

"I heard everything Niles said," he continued with a whinny, "and I think it's safe to say that we're about to experience a little Action, Adventure, and Excitement."

With that, Max snorted noisily and pranced out onto the field of honor, proudly tossing his mane and humming the Notre Dame fight song, while I struggled wildly to hold my lance upright and stay in the saddle.

4

Lining one side of the large open field were long wooden bleachers crowded with cheering spectators. Women waved their scarves and handkerchiefs. Men stood and shouted. From the tops of tall poles, colored banners streamed and flapped in the breeze. On a raised platform behind the bleachers, twenty heralds snapped to attention, pressed golden trumpets to their lips, and blared out a rousing call to arms.

Little League was never like this.

Max tossed his head toward a lone figure mounted on a black steed at the opposite end of the field. "That must be Sir Bevis," he neighed.

It was the Hampshire Mauler, all right, and he looked ready to maul anything that got in his way. His chain mail, shield, sword, and helmet were coal black; and a blood-red tunic dripped from his massive shoulders. Even from a distance, he looked like a killer. I swallowed hard.

"Uh, look, Max," I stammered, "don't you think we should make a break for it before somebody around here gets hurt?"

21

"Relax," said Max, pawing the dirt eagerly. "I happen to know for a fact that jousting is more or less the safest of all the deadly dangerous sports in medieval England."

"Terrific," I said. "How silly of me to worry. I mean, what do I care about a ten-foot-long lance in the gut?"

Before Max could answer, the heralds blasted forth with another jarring fanfare. A hush fell over the crowd, and almost as a single body, they leaned forward in their seats. My heart took a nose dive down into where my tennis shoes should have been.

"Now what?" I hissed.

"No problem," whispered Max. "All you have to do is watch Sir Bevis and do whatever he does."

"Oh, sure," I said. "That's just great. And what if he runs me through with his lance?"

"In that case," said Max, "try not to land on your head. It'll only make matters worse."

I would have let him have it with my spurs, but I didn't have time. I caught some movement out of the corner of my eye, and I looked down the long field through the slits in my helmet. In the center were two narrow lanes separated by a low fence. And at the far end was Sir Bevis—evil, threatening, poised for the kill.

He lowered his lance until it was level and aimed steadily across the field straight at my heart.

What else could I do? I lowered my lance. It wobbled around like crazy.

Abruptly, the trumpets stopped, leaving the shock of silence. In that same instant, Sir Bevis spurred his black stallion and charged forward, his red tunic flapping and the tip of his lance glinting in the sun.

Without a word, Max too leaped forward. We were on a collision course with the Hampshire Mauler.

The muffled thunder of hoofbeats filled the air. Hypnotized, I locked my eyes on the black figure bearing down on us. A cold fear gripped my spine, and I tried desperately to steady my lance.

He was almost upon us—so close that I thought I glimpsed his wild eyes gleaming evilly behind the slits in his black helmet. I braced myself for a terrible blow.

Suddenly, just before I was due to swallow the tip of Sir Bevis's lance, Max opened his mouth, curled back his lips, and at the top of his lungs bellowed: "GERONIMO-O-O-O-O-O-O-O-O-O-O-O-O-O-O-O-O!!!!!"

Sir Bevis's horse gave an alarmed squeal, dug all four hooves into the ground, and skidded to an abrupt halt.

Sir Bevis catapulted out of the saddle, sailed through the air, and fell with a noisy CLANK! onto the field. He was knocked out cold.

Child's play, I thought to myself as Max slowed to a stop and turned around. *This jousting business is mere child's play.*

The crowd went wild. And so they should. It was a brilliant performance.

Of course, from the bleachers, no one heard Max yell or saw that I had never laid a lance on Sir Bevis. All they knew was that on the very first pass, the Hampshire Mauler had been easily unhorsed and lay in a dazed heap on the field. And I was not about to spoil their fun by setting the record straight.

After all, it was the least I could do for Sir Robert while I was occupying his body. Being a hero, I mean. Keeping up the old boy's image in his absence. I'd do the same for anyone.

Max must have felt the same way, because he took plenty of time prancing past the stands, swishing his tail all over the place and snorting fiercely like some kind of wild Arabian stallion.

In the center of the stands was a special section covered with a fringed canopy. As we got closer, I could make out a stern-looking man with a rugged, sun-weathered face sitting under the canopy in a thronelike chair. Beside him was a strikingly pretty girl of about sixteen. She was blushing up a storm and had her eyes cast down at her lap, where she was twisting a long white scarf. Standing beside her, bobbing around gleefully, was a scrawny, gray-haired old woman, who waved us forward like a ground crewman bringing in a jumbo jet. She pointed a bony finger at the girl and winked at me.

Max whispered up at me out of the corner of his mouth. "That man is probably our host, the Earl of Hampshire. And you're in luck, Steve. That girl must be Lady Elizabeth."

"What do you mean, I'm in luck?" I hissed back.

Max didn't answer. Instead, he pulled up in front of the fringed box and, without any warning, bent his front legs and *bowed* before the Earl! The spectators gasped and applauded even more loudly. From everywhere came cries of "Sir Robert! Sir Robert! The Green Falcon!" Flowers flew through the air and fell at our feet. I guess they'd never seen a kneeling horse before.

Unfortunately, I had never been *on* a kneeling horse before. I was caught by surprise and was almost pitched out of the saddle. My lance swung down into the box, nearly nicking the Earl on the nose. He sat back cross-eyed with a startled grunt.

While I struggled to recover, Lady Elizabeth sprang forward and, with lightning speed, tied her white scarf onto the tip of my lance before I could regain my balance and pull it away. Then she fell back into her seat, smiling at me shyly and fluttering her eyelashes. I was glad I was still inside my helmet.

As Max stood up again, Niles suddenly appeared at our side, leading Sir Bevis's black stallion and carrying his black sword. I had read enough about the Middle Ages to know that when a knight wins a jousting match, he wins the other knight's armor and horse, although the loser usually buys back the loot. I guessed that Niles had taken Sir Bevis's sword and horse as a sort of token, since it wouldn't have been polite to strip him of his full armor while he was out cold on the field.

Niles put the sword down and untied Lady Elizabeth's scarf from my lance.

"Ahhhh," he exclaimed in a low voice, " 'twas a gesture of true love." Then, while my hands were full and I couldn't defend myself, he reached up and tucked the scarf inside my tunic—next to my heart. Lady Elizabeth giggled. The old woman skipped from foot to foot, chortling and rubbing her hands together with glee.

I was beginning to wish that Sir Bevis *had* run me through with his lance.

The Earl stood up to make a speech. He threw off his fur-lined cloak and stepped forward, holding up his hand as a signal for silence. The cheers died slowly away.

"Sir Robert Marshall," he boomed for all to hear, "never before have we seen such skill at arms as thou hast shown these past three days. Henceforth, let it be known throughout the land that thou wert the undefeated champion of the Hampshire Tournament in the year of our Lord, twelve hundred and fifty!"

Then, stroking his mustache, he added, "I would count it an honor, Sir Robert, if thou wouldst tarry a while as a guest here at Hampshire Castle. What sayest thou?"

Figuring that Sir Robert would want to accept, I cleared my throat and said, "I'd be happy to, your Earlship."

"Good, good," said the Earl. "Then thou wilt surely join us on the morrow for the hunt. We meet at dawn in the outer bailey."

Without waiting for a reply, he eased himself back into his chair, and the crowd immediately broke into a new storm of cheers and applause. So, while Niles led Sir Bevis's horse back to our tent, Max and I finished parading in front of the stands.

Even when we finally turned and headed back across the field, the thunder of applause followed us. It was great, but I felt a little sad when I realized that within a few short hours we'd be leaving the Middle Ages and winging our way back to our own time. We'd be trading tournaments for TV. It'd be good-bye to glory and hello to hanging around. I heaved a long sigh.

Max, on the other hand, was in high spirits.

"Hey, how about that Geronimo Gimmick?" he whinnied cheerfully. "Pretty terrific, don't you think? And I thought of it *joust* in time." He tittered at his own joke.

"Yeah," I sighed. "Terrific."

"But the best part was that Sir Bevis fell for it. Get it? *Fell* for it!"

"Oh, brother," I muttered, as Max gave a horsy guffaw and trotted briskly across the field toward Sir Robert's tent.

5

No doubt about it, I thought to myself as I entered Sir Robert's spacious, richly furnished tent, these medieval knights really know how to travel in style. As I scanned the elegant décor, I made mental notes so I could pass along a few pointers to our summer counselors at Camp Wongahana about the proper way to outfit a tent.

I noted with approval the thick carpet, the beautifully carved wooden trunks, the wide camp beds with fluffy quilts, the tasteful tapestries, the inviting leather chairs, and the strong oak table set with a slender flagon and several tall goblets made from stag horn and silver. And a squire to wait on me hand and foot—that was a nice touch.

"Sit thee here, Sir Robert," said Niles, bustling around in front of me and pulling a chair forward.

I sat down, and Niles carefully removed my helmet. He parted my hair and clucked over the nasty bump I'd gotten on my head when I fell off Max's back.

"Marry!" he exclaimed. " 'Tis little wonder that thou hast lost thy memory."

He smiled at me with open admiration. "Ah, Sir Robert, only a courageous knight such as thyself could fight such a rousing joust with an injury such as this. Thou art truly a man of iron."

This praise was met with a rude, snickering horse snort. I spun around, and there was Max, nosing his way into the tent.

Niles rushed forward, making shooing motions with his hands. "Out, out, thou sassy horse!" he cried.

Max wasn't impressed. He bared his teeth and snarled, flapping his lips for extra effect. Niles fell back with an astonished squeak.

"It's all right, Niles," I said, trying to keep the peace. "Let's let him in. He can't do any harm."

Niles sniffed primly. "Thou canst carry loyalty to thy horse too far, Sir Robert," he said.

"Says who?" muttered Max as he curled up on the rug.

But he didn't mutter enough. Niles must have heard him because he froze, staring at Max bug-eyed. Then he shook his head hard, as if he were trying to dislodge a mosquito from his nose.

"Nay, nay, 'tis not possible," he mumbled to himself. "Methinks I have been too long in the sun these past three days."

He staggered over to one of the camp beds and collapsed weakly onto it.

Poor Niles. He really was a good-hearted guy. Kind, loyal, trustworthy—everything I always wanted in a squire.

I had just gotten up to find a wet cloth for his forehead, when a strange, chubby man in a long purple robe came dashing into the tent. Catching sight of me, he veered in my direction, tripped over the hem of his robe with both feet, and barely avoided a belly-flop by flailing out with his arm and hooking onto my shoulder.

He steadied himself and stared over at Niles, who had his hand on his head and was moaning, "The sun . . . too much sun . . ."

I figured I'd better say something.

"You must forgive Niles," I whispered. "He's been working too hard and . . . well . . . he's been imagining things. He actually thought he heard my horse talking!"

"Odd's bodkins!" declared the stranger, peeking around my shoulder at the squire. " 'Tis good fortune that I am a doctor. The lad needeth a dash of my pulverized fingernail clippings and a bit of bed rest."

"Oh, you're a *doctor*," I said, noticing for the first time the bulging red bag he was carrying. "Great. Maybe after you've taken care of Niles, you could look at this bump on my head."

" 'Twould be an honor, Sir Robert. But first, allow me to properly introduce myself." He carefully set down his red bag, puffed himself up like a purple balloon, and tossed his shoulder-length hair out of his eyes. "I am Clarence Gathergoods—Doctor, Alchemist, and Barber Extraordinaire."

He bowed gracefully, shoved me into a chair, and poked his finger at the wound on my head.

"Thou hast a bump here, all right," he said. He

fluffed my hair lightly. "And thou couldst use a trim around the sides, too."

Dr. Gathergoods beamed, seeming very pleased with himself for his speedy diagnosis. He patted his large paunch with satisfaction.

"Aye, aye," he declared. "Too much blood in the system. Wc shall have to bleed thee."

"*Bleed* me?" Was this guy a doctor or a vampire? Wcre we in England or Transylvania?

"Why, of course, Sir Robert. Everyone knoweth that in such cases blood-letting is the best cure."

He was wrong. I did not knoweth. If I had knoweth, I would have kept my big mouth shuteth about my bumpeth.

Dr. Gathergoods, however, was unconcerned. He hooked his thumbs in his gold belt and rocked back on his heels. "Just betwixt thee and me and the tent pole, Sir Robert, I am here at Hampshire Castle for a limited time only. I consider this quaint country castle to be but a temporary way station on my pilgrimage to greatness." His eyes glazed slightly. "Aye, 'tis but a matter of time before I shall unlock the secrets of alchemy and shall possess the power to transform ordinary metals to gold!"

He stood staring into space for a few moments and then shook himself out of his dreams and opened his bag. Peering inside, he fluttered his fingers in the air and fussed, "Now where are my leeches? I can never find *anything* in this bag."

Leeches? Whoa and wait a minute here, I thought. *This blood-letting business is bad enough, but leeches? No way. Count me out.*

I watched with a shudder as Dr. Gathergoods reached into his bag and drew out a cloudy jar filled with sleazy, slimy, oozy, wormy, wriggling greenish-black bloodsuckers. I felt sick.

Just about then, Max was seized with a snorting fit. His huge horse body shook, and he sounded as if he were trying to clear his sinuses. I was pretty sure he was laughing.

The doctor proudly set the jar of leeches on the table and then turned his attention back to me. "Now," he wondered, "where shall I apply them? To the left arm? To the right?"

"How about to the horse?" I said, glaring at Max.

Gathergoods broke into hearty chuckles. "Ho, ho, ho. Thou dost tickle me, Sir Robert. And to think that Sir Bevis sayeth that thou hast no sense of humor! But then, Sir Bevis also sayeth that thou hast no honor, guts, or brains."

"He said *what*?"

"No honor, no guts, no brains," repeated the doctor, chortling.

"No kidding," I said, chortling along with him. "So you know good old Sir Bevis, do you?"

"To be sure, Sir Robert. 'Twas on an errand for Sir Bevis that I came to your tent anon. He sent me hither with gold coins to ransom his armor, and he asketh for the speedy return of his sword and his horse."

I sprang to my feet. "What? Speedy return? Then there's no time to lose!" I pressed Sir Bevis's sword into his hand. "Here's the sword. The horse is outside."

"But, but—" sputtered Dr. Gathergoods, "but

32

what of thy blood-letting? 'Tis necessary to—"

"I'm sure you're right, doctor," I interrupted. "Absolutely right. A quart or two of blood off the top and I'd feel much better. But let's be fair. Sir Bevis is probably worrying himself silly wondering what's taking you so long."

I quickly dropped the jar of leeches back into the doctor's bag and thrust it into his hands. He looked bewildered by the sudden change of plan, but finally, reluctantly, he unhooked a leather pouch from his belt and offered it to me.

"Mayhap thou art right, Sir Robert," he said. "Methinks thou wilt find this a fair price."

I accepted the ransom with one hand and propelled him toward the exit with the other.

"But!" The doctor stopped and stood his ground. "Before I go, I feel I should offer thee some sound advice. If thou valuest thy life, do not tarry here at Hampshire Castle. Sir Bevis hath a foul temper and 'tis not for nothing that he is called the Hampshire Mauler."

Niles leaped to his feet. "Fie on Sir Bevis!" he cried. "Sir Robert feareth no man!"

"Calm thyself, good Niles," said Dr. Gathergoods soothingly. "I meant no harm. Thy nerves are frazzled. Here is a vial of the finest pulverized fingernail clippings to be taken with warm wine." He handed a small bottle to Niles and then turned to me with a slight bow. "Till the morrow, Sir Robert."

With that, he waggled his fingers good-bye, tossed his hair out of his eyes, and bustled out of the tent, his purple robe billowing behind.

6

No more than two seconds passed between the time that Dr. Gathergoods swept out of our tent and the time that a wiry old woman scurried in with tremendous energy, her eyes darting every which way and her ragged shawl lurching off one scrawny shoulder. I recognized her right away as the old woman we had seen earlier hovering over Lady Elizabeth in the stands.

"Is he gone?" she demanded in a loud, raspy whisper.

"Who?" I countered.

"Gabby Gathergoods, that's who. Why, I would not trust that old windbag as far as I could throw him."

That wouldn't be far, judging from his weight and her age, whoever she was. Which was my next question.

I smiled politely. "Now let me see, you'd be Miss . . . Miss . . ."

She cocked her head to one side and grinned up at me. About half her teeth were missing.

"Who be I? Who be I?" she crowed, swatting me playfully on the arm. "I be Agnes Longtooth, Lady

Elizabeth's lady-in-waiting, as thou well knowest, thou sly fox."

"Agnes," Niles broke in urgently, "takest thou not a grave risk in coming here without the Earl's permission?"

"Aye, Niles," she said, nodding vigorously, "we all be in great danger. Thou knowest how closely the Earl doth guard his daughter's reputation. Not to mention Sir Bevis. He is a jealous one, he is. Have a care, Sir Robert. Sir Bevis is after thy blood.

"*But*," she continued with a big delighted grin, " 'tis a risk well taken. For 'tis a risk taken for Love. I have a *message*."

She sidled up to me sideways like a crab and squeezed my elbow intimately. "For *thee*, Sir Robert. From *Lady Elizabeth*."

Uh-oh. Trouble. I felt a stab of panic and looked to Niles for help, but he had discovered something extremely fascinating about the tip of his boot and was giving it his full attention.

"M'lady sayeth," crooned Agnes, drawing out each word, "that she doth find thee a right brave knight, most fearless and dashing, and comely to look upon." Agnes snickered noisily into her hand and then leered up at me. "Eh? Eh?" she urged, jabbing me in the ribs with her razor-sharp elbow. "And hast thou not a *message* for m'lady?"

I was as speechless as Agnes was toothless, but she just kept staring at me with her bright, beady eyes, waiting for an answer. I broke out in a cold sweat, and my knees trembled slightly.

Stalling for time, I reached into my tunic, pulled

out a handkerchief, and wiped the sweat from my forehead.

I almost jumped out of my skin when Agnes greeted this simple act with a loud cackle of triumph. "Ah-ha! Enough said, Sir Robert! I will deliver thy message."

Still crowing with glee, she darted out of the tent, ducking and weaving as she went.

Did I miss something? I shot a questioning glance at Max, but he looked as puzzled as I was.

Niles, however, coughed delicately, caught my eye, and gave me an admiring grin.

"Thou shalt never cease to amaze me, Sir Robert," he said. "Not only art thou a master in the arts of war, but thou art a master in the arts of love as well."

"Huh?" I croaked.

" 'Tis no use pretending, sire. I saw the whole thing. Without uttering a word that might compromise the honor of Lady Elizabeth, thou didst draw her scarf from the honored place over thy heart and touch it, as if in sacred vow, to thy forehead."

Astonished, I stared down at the handkerchief in my hand. He was right. It wasn't a handkerchief. It was Lady Elizabeth's white scarf!

7

After that, things moved fast.

First, I ditched Lady Elizabeth's scarf. For good, I hoped.

Second, Niles ate the powdered fingernail clippings. I turned a sickly green and Max turned away, rolling his eyes and flabbering his lips.

Third, Niles helped me out of my chain mail and into a loose-fitting tunic, poured me a goblet of wine, and rushed out to make arrangements for tomorrow's hunt.

And finally, Max and I went exploring.

"Now's our chance," I said, jumping up. "Let's have a look around before the time machine yanks us back home."

Max stuck his head out of the tent. "Sounds like something's going on over by the castle," he whinnied. "Let's go."

We scrambled out of the tent and hurried toward the castle. And when we rounded the last tent, we weren't disappointed. Along the outer bank of the moat, a real, live medieval fair had been set up to celebrate the last day of the Hampshire Tournament.

Dozens of open-air booths lined the moat, and in front of each booth was a large, noisy crowd. There were puppet shows and magic shows and trained monkeys and gypsy fortune-tellers. And all kinds of sports and games and lots of people selling strange-looking foods.

In high spirits, Max and I plunged into the throng. I ate my fill of venison and fresh-baked bread; joined a cheering circle at a sawdust ring and won a wager on a wrestling match; and paid a gold coin to do the polka with a dancing bear.

As the afternoon wore on, we happened onto a group of archers who were competing against each other. With deadly seriousness and without speaking a word, they took turns shooting at a single target that had been placed about a hundred yards away, on the edge of the moat. We watched for several minutes, but even though every arrow hit the target, not one had yet hit the bull's-eye.

It wasn't long before one of the stout bowmen recognized me and stepped forth.

"Greetings, Green Falcon," he said, bowing respectfully. "Wouldst thou care to try thy hand with the longbow? Thou art known to have few equals as an archer."

Max gave me a warning nudge, but I knew I had nothing to worry about. The fact is that I was a bit of a whiz when I took archery in gym class.

"Yea, verily," said I, striding gallantly to the shooting line, with Max at my heels. "Many is the arrow I have shot in the name of Justice and Truth. And now I shall shoot yet another in the name of Sport."

Like wildfire, the word spread that Sir Robert was about to demonstrate his skill at archery, and within moments a large crowd had gathered round. If only Coach Collins could see me now.

I tested the wind with my finger, then nodded for the bow. With something of a swagger, I set my feet firmly, fitted an arrow, and drew back the string. A hush fell over the crowd.

For three seconds . . . five . . . ten . . . I stood motionless, a slight sneer on my face, sighting down the arrow to the exact center of the bull's-eye. No one breathed.

At twenty seconds I released the string.

Straight and true flew the noble shaft.

Well, all right, maybe it was just a little wide of the mark. And, okay, maybe just a little high and far.

The arrow struck high against the castle wall, shattered noisily, and fell in pieces into the moat.

"Rats!" quoth I.

"Yea, verily," muttered Max under his breath.

Fortunately, the crowd thought I was joking, and I wasn't going to tell them any different. I laughed as heartily as everyone else, slapping backs and shaking hands, while Max stood back, shaking his head. It's hard to tell with a horse, but I think he was disgusted.

By now it was getting dark, so Max and I headed back to Sir Robert's tent. Along the way, Max turned to me with a frown on his long horse face.

"Steve," he said, "I'm worried. According to my calculations, we've been here in the Middle Ages for a lot more than three hours, and we should be home by now."

Motor-Mind was at it again. I'd been hoping he

wouldn't notice that little fact. "Relax," I said. "We just lost track of time, that's all."

"Yeah," said Max darkly, "just so long as time didn't lose track of *us*."

If he was going to worry that much about it, I decided, maybe I'd better confess. So I told him how I had changed our Length-of-Stay from three hours to eight hours. Luckily, Max was so relieved to hear that the time machine hadn't broken down that he forgot to be mad at me.

"You're *sure* you changed it to eight hours?" he asked as we arrived at Sir Robert's tent.

"Sure, I'm sure," I said. "And if we just get a little sleep, by the time we wake up we'll be back home in ye old clubhouse, safe and sound."

We ducked inside the tent. Niles was already sacked out, snoring softly. I was pretty tired myself. So, yawning, I flopped down onto my cot, pulled the fluffy cover up to my shoulders, and fell fast asleep.

It's hard work being a hero.

8

I woke up the next morning in our clubhouse back home, rested up and ready to go. The early dawn light filtered in through the yellow canvas, and from somewhere in the distance came the call of a hunting horn. Max whinnied good morning.

Hold it. Hooooolllld it! My razor-sharp reflexes sensed that something was not quite right. I closed my eyes and started over.

But when I opened them again, it was all too clear. We were not back home. We were still in the Middle Ages, Max was still a horse, and I was still a knight— handsome, dashing, heroic, known far and wide as Champion of the Hampshire Tournament, adored by one and all.

Oh, well, I thought, *things could be worse*.

"Ah, thou art awake, Sir Robert," chirped a cheery voice. It was Niles, setting out a light breakfast of bread and honey. "There is time for but a quick snack, sire. The huntsmen are this very minute gathering in the outer bailey. I will go and see that they await thee." He hurried out, calling over his shoulder, "Make haste!"

Max and I were alone. Naturally, I was just a smidgen worried that Max might be mad at me on account of how we were still in the Middle Ages, and he was still wearing a tail and four hooves. After all, I was the one who had talked him into using Flybender's time machine in the first place.

I glanced over at him. But he was just standing there, looking at me with his big horse eyes. He didn't *look* mad. Which was good, because I never like to have someone mad at me if he weighs more than a thousand pounds.

"You'd better hurry," said Max, pawing the ground eagerly. "The hunt's about to begin."

"What's this?" I said, surprised. "Aren't you even worried about how we're stuck here in the Middle Ages?"

"Sure," Max said airily. "But we're here, so we might as well make the best of it. Besides, before you got up, I ambled over to the outer bailey, and I think this hunt might be good for a few laughs."

Was this my old friend Max, three-time winner of the Worry-Wart Award? I should have known right then that he was up to something.

But before I had time to get suspicious, there came again the distant, haunting call of the hunting horn, and now we could hear the restless baying of hounds. The Hunt! My spine tingled with excitement.

"TALLYHO!" Max cried, and he trotted out of the tent.

In a flash, I leaped to my feet, grabbed a green cloak, and followed on his heels.

I had no idea where we were going. That is, I had

no idea where the outer bailey was. It turned out that the castle had two rings of walls, one within the other. The large courtyard just inside the outer walls was called the outer bailey. The smaller paved courtyard, inside the inner walls, was the inner bailey.

Across the drawbridge we went—me jogging alongside Max—through the arch of the main gate and into the dusty courtyard. There, in the midst of a bunch of squabbling chickens, waddling ducks, and rooting pigs, the hunting party was gathering. About thirty men and women were there already. The hounds were darting among the nervous horses, barking happily.

Even Lady Elizabeth was there, with a falcon perched on her gloved wrist. Agnes Longtooth stood beside her, steadying her horse.

Although they were at the far end of the courtyard, and I was nonchalantly trying to hide behind Max, old Agnes spotted me. Instantly, she whooped and pointed, hopping from foot to foot, and then cupped her hands around her mouth and yodeled across the courtyard. "Sir Rooooooobert! Oh, Sir Rooooooobert!" She waved wildly. Lady Elizabeth smiled and nodded a shy hello.

I nodded back.

Suddenly, a cold shadow fell over me and at the same moment I heard a threatening, bearish grunt behind me. I spun around with a start.

Glowering down at me was a gorilla of a man—a man with huge hunched shoulders, long muscular arms, and deep-set animal eyes. He wore his wiry black hair in a tight roll around his face, and a blood-red cloak off one shoulder. His thick lips quivered with hatred.

It was the Hampshire Mauler.

"Keep thee away from Lady Elizabeth, knave," he snarled, clenching his meaty hands into fists, "or I will batter thee to bits and throw thee into the moat as fish feed!"

As I was wondering whether I should teach this big bully a lesson in manners, then and there, or whether I should run for my life instead, the Earl of Hampshire strode up and clapped a hand on Sir Bevis's shoulder.

"Hold, Sir Bevis!" he commanded. "What means this uncouth talk? It doth thee no honor to bear a grudge against Sir Robert for winning the tourney. Put aside thy ill feelings and accept Sir Robert as thine own true friend. 'Tis my wish."

Sir Bevis shot me a piercing look. "What grudge is there to bear, m'lord?" he growled. "'Twas a fair-fought fight, was it not, Sir Robert?"

Was it my imagination, or was there a note of suspicion there?

Sir Bevis leaped effortlessly into the saddle and reined his horse around. I must have imagined it.

At a sign from the Earl, the hunting horn was again sounded—two clear blasts that echoed off the stone walls. A shout went up as everyone mounted. Then, with the Earl and me in the lead, the hunting party spurred their horses, galloped out the main gate, and clattered across the drawbridge.

The Earl turned to me and shouted to be heard over the sound of hoofbeats. "Sir Robert, I know that a falconer as famous as thyself will choose to join the hawking party. I will see thee anon. Good hunting!"

With that, the Earl and half the riders peeled off and galloped away toward the distant hills in search of deer, while Max and I joined the hawkers as they rode toward a thick, sprawling forest.

A hawking party! I thought with soaring spirits. How medieval-ly can you get? I glanced quickly around. About half the riders in our group had falcons—fierce hawks trained to bring down other birds—tied to their heavily gloved wrists. Not even the fact that Sir Bevis had joined our group could dampen my enthusiasm.

As we came to the edge of the forest, the horses were reined to a walk, and the hunting party fanned out. Each rider picked his own path through the dense, leafy undergrowth. I sat back in the saddle and enjoyed the coolness of the shade.

Until, that is, I realized that Max was making a beeline for Lady Elizabeth.

I sat up like a shot and tugged on the reins. Max ignored me. Leaning over, I whispered furiously in his ear, "Just where do you think you're going, horse brain?"

"Oh, I just thought I'd trot over to Lady Elizabeth and give you a chance to be neighborly," he neighed innocently.

Max was up to something, I was pretty sure of that. He probably thought he could get even with me for writing that love letter to Dawn Sharington for him. But he had made a big mistake. He had put me on guard. Instantly, my brain snapped to attention. My keen senses went on full alert. My eyes narrowed watchfully. And yet outwardly, I remained calm and composed.

A knight knows no fear.

As we pulled up alongside Lady Elizabeth, I gave her a polite nod. She looked pleased and nodded back modestly. So far, so good.

Then it happened.

As we passed through a dark, shady patch of forest, Max broke the silence. In an excellent imitation of my own voice, he spoke to Lady Elizabeth.

"My darling Elizabeth. How my heart doth yearn for thee!"

Lady Elizabeth practically swooned out of her saddle. I practically croaked.

"Oh, Sir *Robert*!" she cried breathlessly. "I . . . I . . . I had no *idea*!" She turned her face away, overcome with embarrassment.

I made a strangling noise. I was pretty overcome myself.

"I am thy devoted slave for life, fair lady," added Max. "Do with me what thou wilt."

Lady Elizabeth tittered up and down the scale, shielding her eyes, blushing a bright pink.

I gnashed my teeth. *This horse*, I told myself, *is done for*.

"My life is a torment without thee, my dearest! Wilt thou be mine?"

Yeeeeeeeech! My face was burning. I hunched my shoulders and tried to slide down in my seat, but that doesn't work very well when you're high in the saddle. It was more than I could stand. I had to get out of there.

I gave Max a loud THWACK! on the rump, but instead of galloping away like I hoped he would, he capered forward a few steps, and then launched into a ridiculous dance routine. He started with a series of high-stepping prances and prissy little kicks with his hind legs and finished up with a stiff-legged pogo-stick number that rattled my teeth.

Lady Elizabeth dissolved into gales of giggles. She thought I was showing off.

Just as I was getting ready to fall off Max's back, pretending to have a heart attack, I heard the sound of a horse crashing through the underbrush. A moment later Sir Bevis joined us.

I never thought I'd be glad to see the Hampshire Mauler, but just then I felt as if the United States Cavalry had arrived, bugles blaring, just in the nick of time.

I was so grateful that I put on my best British accent, grinned at him, and said, "I say, Sir Bevis, old chap, jolly fine day for a hunt, what?"

He sneered a reply that I didn't quite catch. But it sounded suspiciously like, "Button thy lip, varlet!"

This guy had all the charm of a stinkbug.

9

For a while Lady Elizabeth, Sir Bevis, and I rode together in strained silence. Soon the forest thinned, and we came out on the marshy bank of a wide river. Turning north, we followed the river upstream.

Lady Elizabeth gently removed the hood that had been tied over her falcon's head to keep him calm during the ride through the forest. It seemed like a good time to break the tension with a little small talk.

"Nice bird you got there," I commented.

"Aye," gushed Lady Elizabeth proudly. "Is he not beautiful?" She held him out at arm's length for me to see.

He was quite a bird, all right. My guess was that in the grim game of death, this falcon was a winner. He was arrogant. Alert. With cruel, piercing eyes, and long, curving claws. The slow twist of his head was cool and calculating. He had the air of a born killer.

"What's his name?" I asked.

"Fluff-ums," she said.

"Fluff-ums?"

The falcon turned his murderous, unblinking eyes

on me, as if it were *my* fault his name was Fluff-ums.
He flexed his gleaming claws—claws a grizzly bear
would have been proud of.

"But," continued Lady Elizabeth, "he is very sen-
sitive and will not tolerate another person besides myself." She tickled Fluff-ums under the chin and cooed,
"Wilt thou, thou wittle wascal?"

The falcon never took his eyes off me.

Sir Bevis, who had been watching this scene with
interest, broke in with an oily smile. "Why dost thou
not allow Sir Robert to test thy bird, Lady Elizabeth?
'Tis said that in the sport of falconry, he has no equal."

"Nay, nay," said Lady Elizabeth, flustered. " 'Tis
too dangerous. Since he was but a tiny fledgling, Fluff-
ums hath known no hand but mine own. 'Twould be
nothing for him to bite off a finger or put out the eyes
of one who is unfamiliar to him."

Sir Bevis gave a hearty laugh that rang harsh and
hollow. "Thou forgetest, m'lady, that 'twas Sir Robert's uncanny skill with falcons that earned him the
name Green Falcon." He turned to me. "Thou art not
afeared of Fluff-ums, art thou, Sir Robert?"

He watched me closely with his crafty snake eyes,
waiting—hoping—for a sign of weakness. That two-bit
turkey was trying to use a hawk to make me look like a
chicken. Well, it wasn't going to work. Little did he
know that I once recaptured my little sister's pet para-
keet, Petunia, *with my bare hands.*

"Are you kidding?" I said with breezy confidence.
"I love this little killer." I held out my hand as an
invitation for Fluff-ums to climb aboard.

"Truly thou art a brave knight," said Lady Elizabcth. She smiled up at me as she put her gloved wrist next to my unprotected one.

Slowly and deliberately, Fluff-ums locked first one set of talons and then the other around my arm, smirking evilly. His eyes never left my face for an instant. Now what? I wondered.

When in doubt, try flattery. I smiled lovingly at the falcon, eyeball to eyeball, and said cheerily, "You're a spunky little birdy, aren't you, old fella?"

I guess I said the wrong thing. Maybe I should have said he was a spunky *big* birdy. Fluff-ums uttered an enraged screech and lunged for my nose.

I flung my arm wildly away from my face with all of Sir Robert's strength. Still screeching, the falcon soared away into the sky.

We watched in stunned silence as he climbed higher and higher. Just as I was wondering what sort of horrible medieval torture the Earl would arrange for me when he found out I had lost his daughter's beloved wittle wascal, Fluff-ums folded his wings and plunged into a dive. It was then that we saw the duck rising up from the river. He never knew what hit him. Fluff-ums struck hard and then followed his kill to the earth.

Arrogantly, he perched atop his fallen prey.

All in all, I prefer parakeets.

10

Shortly after Fluff-ums's spectacular flight, we joined the rest of the hawking party along the river bank. Right away, Lady Elizabeth exclaimed to everyone about how I had tamed her precious Fluff-ums and had made him bring down a duck on the very first try. She said Fluff-ums respected me. He loved me. He looked up to me as a father.

I guess Fluff-ums was well known to everyone there, because they all seemed very impressed. It didn't do any good to protest, either. As far as they were concerned, I must be the World's Greatest Falcon Expert.

Naturally, they all wanted some of my expert advice. For the rest of the morning and into the afternoon, as the hunt went on, people kept galloping over to me to ask "just one more question" of the great Green Falcon.

"Good Sir Robert," asked one lady excitedly, "what diet dost thou recommend for the raising of a champion falcon?"

"Boiled beets," I said, taking a wild guess. "But mark my words: *no turnips.*"

She thanked me eight or nine times and galloped away.

A short, round-faced man wanted to know what he could do about his falcon, which insisted on carrying off its prey instead of waiting for its master.

I didn't have the faintest idea, but I had to say something.

"Sir," I said, "communication is the answer. Have you ever actually sat down with your falcon and talked this thing out?"

The round-faced man looked confused. "Nay," he stammered. "I have not."

"Then do so!" I said heartily. "You'll be glad you did. After all, if you can't talk to your falcon, then who can you talk to?"

I slapped him on the back and gave him a we-falconers-understand-such-things sort of smile. He nodded uncertainly and rode off slowly. I noticed that he wore a puzzled expression on his face for the rest of the day.

Meanwhile, Sir Bevis wore an expression of burning hatred. All day long he hung back from the group, dangerously quiet. Even when we stopped for a picnic, he sat off to one side. Behind those cold, flinty eyes he looked as if he were masterminding a murder. Mine.

Late that afternoon, the hawking party started slowly back toward the castle. It had been a long day and everyone was tired, so we rode along without much talking.

Suddenly, Max trotted out ahead of the group.

"Did you feel something just now?" he asked me in a low, urgent voice. "Sort of a dizzy feeling?"

"No," I said. "Why? What's the matter?"

"Something funny's going on," he said. "That's the third time today I've felt the same dizzy feeling. And you know what's weird about it? It's exactly like the feeling I had back in the clubhouse when the time machine was just starting to work."

"But it can't be the time machine," I said, ducking under a low branch as we turned away from the river and entered the forest. "If it were trying to bring us back, I'd feel dizzy, too."

Max thought for a minute. "I don't think it's trying to bring us back," he said finally. "You know what I think? I think the time machine may be losing its grip on me."

A slight chill went up my spine. "What do you mean, *losing its grip*?"

"Well," said Max, talking slowly like he does when he's reasoning something out, "remember back in the clubhouse when you pulled the ON lever? You were standing right next to the time machine, but I was way across the room and halfway out the door. Maybe I was too far away for the time machine to get a good, firm hold on me."

"Maybe," I said doubtfully. "But what if you're right and it *does* lose its hold on you? What would happen?"

"I'm not sure," said Max, "and I don't particularly want to find out, either. I suppose I could go into limbo or something. Or end up floating around in time. I don't know. But anyway, I guess there's not much we can do about it. I just hope Professor Flybender knew more about time machines than you know about falcons, that's all."

Before I could answer, a branch cracked loudly

somewhere in the forest behind us. Max and I looked around. A huge, hulking form on a black horse loomed out of the dark shadows. It was Sir Bevis. He had separated from the hunting party and seemed to be following us at a distance. Even in the gloom of the forest, I could make out his brutal, bloodthirsty leer. His thick lips were pulled back, and his teeth gleamed in the darkness.

"Keep an eye on Sir Bevis," Max warned. "He's up to something!"

Actually, Sir Bevis was keeping *his* eye on *me*. All during our ride back through the forest and across the broad meadow below the castle, I felt as if I were being tracked by a six-foot-tall rattlesnake.

Then it happened. Just as Max and I reached the drawbridge, I heard hoofbeats approaching and glanced back over my shoulder. There was Sir Bevis, closing in on us fast. His face was black with rage. Suddenly, there was a flash of cold steel.

"Max!" I yelled. "He's got a knife!"

Max thought fast. He hit the brakes, stuck out one leg, and tripped Sir Bevis's horse when he pulled alongside. As Sir Bevis and his horse veered sharply toward the edge of the drawbridge, I took careful aim and gave Sir Bevis a hefty assist with the flat of my foot.

Over the edge they tumbled. Airborne. The sky above, the moat below.

For a moment or two, things didn't look too bad for Sir Bevis. In fact, it looked as if he had a very respectable swan dive going. But at the last minute he chickened out. With a husky little scream, the Hampshire Mauler hit the water doing a cannonball.

His horse did more of a belly-flop, its legs spread out wide and flat.

The hawking party reined to a stop and exploded into loud laughter. Within seconds, people began streaming out of the castle to see what all the excitement was about.

Sir Bevis, sputtering and cursing, grabbed his free-floating saddle as it drifted by, struggled up onto it, and began paddling for shore. On a surfboard he might have looked good, but on a saddle he didn't. Everybody thought he was hilarious. Lady Elizabeth laughed so hard I thought she was going to fall off her horse.

Suddenly, the Earl appeared on top of the castle wall. He took one look down into the moat and almost swallowed his mustache.

"By'r Lady, Sir Bevis!" he roared. "What means this foolery? Get thee out of that moat. Thou lookest a silly ass!" And, shaking his head with disgust, he disappeared back behind the wall.

Still snickering, the crowd slowly broke up and headed into the castle. I slipped off Max's back and joined them on foot. There is something very undignified about riding a horse who has a case of the jiggling giggles.

11

We had no sooner passed through the archway into the inner bailey than something strange happened to Max. There he was, chuckling happily to himself, when he jerked to a stop and was seized with a long, violent shudder. It began way out at the tip of his nostrils and finished up way out at the tip of his tail. But then, just as suddenly, with a toss of his head and a flick of his tail, he seemed to be perfectly normal again.

Seemed normal, sure. That was because I was so busy thinking about Sir Bevis's wide-eyed expression just before he hit the water that I didn't notice that Max was not his usual self.

I draped my arm around his tall shoulder and said, "Congratulations on the fast thinking back there on the drawbridge, partner. What's your code name for this one going to be? The Cannonball Caper?"

Max didn't answer. Surprised, I stepped back, took a good look at him, and saw that his eyes were glazed, as if he were a million miles away. I reached up and rapped on his forehead.

"Anything going on up there?" I asked.

Still no answer. No wisecrack. No nothing. Just a blank, horsy stare. And that's when it hit me. That's when I realized the terrible truth. *Max was gone!*

I was stunned. I gaped at the horse, but he just stood there, slowly swishing his tail back and forth. If Max wasn't here, then where was he? Probably nowhere, that's where. Lost in the middle of nothingness. Floating in time, just as he had predicted. And it was all my fault.

If only I hadn't turned the time machine on while Max was halfway out of the clubhouse!

We were both in el big-o trouble now. Max was drifting around somewhere, and I was stranded here in the Middle Ages—*alone.*

In my own quiet sort of way, I began to panic. But just as I was about to run back out and fling myself into the moat with Sir Bevis, I spotted my squire approaching.

"Sir Robert!" he cried, a big grin on his face. "I have just come from the moat. Odd's fish! Didst thou see Sir Bevis upon his saddle? Didst thou see him paddle? Marry! Methinks I have—"

Niles stopped in midsentence. He swayed gently on his feet for a few seconds, like a tree in a light breeze. Then his eyelids flickered, his knees buckled, and he fainted in a heap on the stone pavement.

First Max and now Niles? What was going on?

"Get the doctor!" I shouted to a passing stable boy. "My squire has fainted!"

The stable boy took off in search of the doctor. He must have found him right away, because within minutes Dr. Gathergoods was running toward me across the courtyard, waving his hands over his head, his purple robes flapping. Pigs and chickens scattered in his wake.

"Courage, good sir!" he shouted as he came. "Clarence Gathergoods cometh!"

Niles was slowly coming to, shaking his head, still dazed. Dr. Gathergoods knelt beside him.

"What happened?" Niles murmured faintly.

"Do not move, poor lad," said the doctor soothingly. "Sir Robert and I will carry thee to thy new quarters."

"What new quarters?" I asked.

"Why, thy room in the base of yon tower, sire. All the other knights have returned whence they came and 'twould be unseemly for thee, a guest of the Earl, to remain camped outside the castle walls in a tent."

"Oh, right," I agreed. "Most unseemly."

Dr. Gathergoods bent over and took hold of Niles's arms. I grabbed his legs. Together we lifted him and slowly, awkwardly, carried him toward one of the round towers along the inner walls. The doctor wasn't holding up his end very well, and Niles sagged heavily between us. His backside bumped along the uneven stones.

"I think I can walk now," he groaned weakly.

"Nonsense," said Dr. Gathergoods generously. "I would not hear of it." He let go of Niles with one hand so that he could open the thick wooden door to our room. Niles's head conked loudly against the doorstep.

"Really, I think I can make it by myself," Niles protested, trying to struggle free.

"Nay, nay. 'Tis best for thee to save thy strength,"

advised the doctor, backing through the door. Unfortunately, he misjudged the clearance, and the squire's shoulder slammed hard against the door frame.

Niles opened his mouth to cry out, but just then Gathergoods tripped, stumbled backward across the room, and dropped his half of Niles altogether. Niles's head crashed squarely into the middle of a chess set arranged on a low table. Pawns, bishops, and queens scattered across the floor.

Niles made a whimpering sound. "Can we stop now?" he pleaded.

Dr. Gathergoods knelt by his patient's side. "There now," he said cheerily. "Are we all nice and comfy?" He gestured for me to lower Niles's legs to the ground, which left Niles sort of balanced on his back on the chess table. "Pour me some wine if thou wilt, Sir Robert. Poor Niles needeth refreshment."

I glanced quickly around the small round room, lit by the late afternoon sun as it streamed in through the high, slit windows. All of Sir Robert's things were there, including his flagon of red wine. I filled a cup and passed it to the doctor.

Dr. Gathergoods winked at me and unhooked a small pouch from his belt. Making sure Niles couldn't see what he was doing, he sprinkled about three tablespoons of pink powder from the pouch into the wine. He swished it around and then thrust the cup under Niles's nose.

"Drink this, lad," he coaxed, "and thou wilt be a new man for it."

Niles, thinking it was only wine, took the brew and gulped it down. It must have been pretty strong stuff, because just after the last swallow, he shuddered horribly, crossed his eyes, and burped.

"What *was* that?" he gasped.

"Powdered bat's blood, bits o' mummy, and crushed garlic," said the doctor proudly. " 'Twill give thee strength and long life."

Niles clutched his stomach, and his tongue lolled out of his mouth. I thought he was going to throw up, but he didn't.

"Aye," continued Gathergoods modestly, " 'tis said that my potions are without equal. But truly, they are but a small sample of my talents."

"Not small enough," Niles squeaked feebly.

"My true greatness doth lie in other realms. Why, in my secret laboratory I have ancient Arabian texts, which will allow me to solve the mysteries of magic and alchemy. Soon I shall have great powers and shall transform common metals to gold, foretell the future, fly through the air on magical carpets! Aye, and even Time itself will do my bidding!"

For a few moments he stood there, captured by the wonder of his vision. Then he snapped out of it, looking slightly flustered, as if he had said too much.

"Forsooth," he said, " 'tis late. I must be off." He gave Niles a fatherly whack on his injured shoulder, bowed to me, and rushed out of the room.

Painfully, Niles motioned me to his side. He was still sprawled out on his back across the low table, his legs dangling off, heels on the floor. Raising his head with an effort, he reached out shakily and grasped my shoulder.

"The next time I faint . . ." he said, breathing hard

and wincing from his wounds. "The next time I faint," he began again, "do me a favor, will you? Just put me in a trunk, tie the trunk up with a thousand feet of chain, put it in a cart, cover it with hay, and smuggle me out of the country. And if you should happen to run into Dr. Gathergoods along the way, tell him that I transformed myself into a golden peach pit and was carried off to Miami Beach by the Wicked Witch of the West."

Miami Beach? The Wicked Witch of the West? This didn't sound like Niles. I mean, shouldn't there have been a "methinks" or a "forsooth" in there somewhere? Somehow this sounded more like the good old twentieth-century U.S. of A. than it did like medieval England.

"Max!" I cried. "Is that you?"

"Of course it's me, or what's left of me," he said, trying to get up. "And what I'd like to know is how are we going to get out of the Middle Ages before Dr. Gathergoods finishes me off?"

It was Max, all right. The old worry wart himself. I guess the time machine had lost its grip on him for only a minute. And when it got hold of him again, it must have missed its target and refocused him a few feet away—right into Niles.

"Crazy doctor," Max was grumbling, ". . . *powdered bat's blood* . . ."

I was never so glad to hear anyone grumble in my life.

12

"You know, Max," I said, grinning, "you seem to be moving up in the world. First a horse and now a squire. Who knows, you could get to be a knight someday." I flexed my knightly muscles. "Or who knows," I added, "maybe a duck."

"Gee, thanks," said Max, struggling to his feet. "But actually, a duck would be fine. At least then Dr. Gathergoods wouldn't notice me."

He checked himself over and decided he didn't have any serious injuries. It was weird watching Niles's face and seeing Niles's clothes and everything, and knowing it was really Max inside.

He picked up a mirror and examined his new face. "I don't know," he said. "This business of changing bodies all the time could get pretty upsetting. I mean, I led a more stable life as a horse. Get it? A *stable* life!" He chuckled to himself. "Just a little horse humor there," he added.

I rolled my eyes up to the ceiling, wondering how long I was going to be saddled with horse humor, when suddenly I remembered Max's little stunt while we were on the hunt. Meaning, of course, those sickening "how my heart doth yearn for thee" speeches he made to Lady Elizabeth for me. Just because I never got a chance to clobber him as a horse didn't mean that I couldn't clobber him as a squire.

"Mercy me," I said pleasantly. "I think I plumb forgot to thank you for all those nice, mushy speeches you made for me this morning on the hunt. How can I ever repay you?"

I went for him, but he dodged behind a large leather chair. He grinned at me over the high back.

"What are friends for?" he said, shrugging. "Besides, everything that Dawn Sharington and I mean to each other, I owe to you. I'm just tickled that I was able to return the favor. And may I say that you and Lady Elizabeth make a *lovely* couple!"

I lunged. Max dived. The chair went over with a crash, and so did we.

There was a loud knock at the door.

"Come in," I called, my arms locked around Max's foot.

The door swung open and in strode the Earl of Hampshire. He looked down at us, shocked. Max and I scrambled to our feet, and together we righted the chair.

"Heh, heh," I said, smiling weakly. "My foolish squire did trip upon yon chair, and I did seize his foot to break his fall."

"Yea, verily," said Max. "Wouldst thou like some wine, m'lord?"

Luckily, the Earl seemed too busy with his own thoughts to notice that my explanation was a wee bit stupid. He accepted a goblet of wine and sank down into the leather chair.

"Thank thee, Niles," he said to Max. He took a little sip, decided he liked it, and then put the rest away in a single swallow. "I came to tell thee, Sir Robert, that thy dinner will be brought to thee here, for as thou knowest, the great hall is even now being prepared for my daughter's birthday feast on the morrow. Aye," he said thoughtfully, pulling at his mustache, "my little Elizabeth will be sixteen. Marrying age."

His dark, solemn eyes fell on me as he said this. I gauged the distance between my chair and the door.

"But 'tis not of this that I wish to speak," he added.

Whew!

"I have been watching thee, Sir Robert, and I like thy mettle. Thou art a champion at jousting, archery, and falconry, and 'tis said that no sane man will cross swords with thee willingly. For this reason, I have chosen to share my dream with thee. And a noble and valiant dream it is—a dream worthy of knights gallant!"

His eyes flashed, and suddenly, he sprang to his feet and began pacing around the small room like a caged lion. His fur-lined cloak swirled when he turned, and his deep voice boomed.

"Sir Robert, I mean to join the Crusades!"

He paused to get my reaction. I was impressed.

"Canst thou not picture it, Sir Robert?" continued the Earl, with a faraway look in his eyes. "Thee and me, side by side as we fight to free the Holy Land from the Arab infidels! Thee and me, side by side in the dust and din of battle, thrilling to the sound of sword against sword! And, God willing, thee and me standing triumphant within the walls of holy Jerusalem!"

He paused again. I was stunned. He and me? In a real, live, genuine *war*? No, thanks. Count me out.

Max cleared his throat politely. "Er . . . pardon me, m'lord, but just how is the Crusade going? Have you had any news from the front?"

"Aye, friend Niles. At last report, I did hear that good King Louis of France, his three brave brothers, and his army of fifteen thousand stout-hearted men were deep in Egypt. There they have met with defeat at every turn. And those who have not died in battle are suffering from disease and starvation." He turned to me with enthusiasm. "Well, what sayest thou, Sir Robert? Wilt thou join me in this noble quest?"

I broke out in a sweat. How do you say "No way, José!" to an earl and survive? I racked my brain for something to say. Then, suddenly, I remembered what my great-uncle Dexter always says: "If you can't convince 'em, confuse 'em." I decided to try it.

I pounded my fist on the table, rattling the chessmen and nearly upsetting the flagon of wine.

"M'lord," I said, speaking with great fire and conviction, "thou hast asked me a question fair and true, and I shall answer thee forthrightly and forthwith. Hark ye! Mark ye! The House of Representatives! I speak, m'lord, of first base, second base, third base, and—forsooth—*home plate*! *Zounds!* For a farthing I would leave my heart in San Francisco. Nay, nay, a thousand times, nay. Dracula and his band of ruthless ruffians *shall not bob for apples*! Ho! Therefore, wherefore, I do say it so!"

The Earl's mouth hung slightly open. "Huh?" he croaked.

Max leaped forward and bowed before the Earl.

"Sir Robert sayeth," he said, "that he is deeply honored by thy request. It is, however, a most important decision, and he therefore asketh that you grant to him a measure of time in which to consider the offer more carefully."

I couldn't have said it better myself.

"Certainly," said the Earl, nodding with approval. He opened the door. "I shall look for thy answer within the fortnight, Sir Robert. Until tomorrow's feast, then." He smiled and strode out of the room.

We gazed after him. *The next time I see my great-uncle Dexter*, I thought to myself, *I'll have to ask him what you're supposed to do* after *you've confused 'em.* After all, Max might not be around next time.

Max and I looked at each other—and suddenly we burst out laughing. "*Home plate?*" whooped Max, punching me. We laughed so hard we couldn't talk. Max stepped on a loose chess piece and went down. I collapsed next to him, gasping.

"*Zounds!*" I said weakly.

13

An hour and a half later, Max and I were sitting alone in our cozy room, surrounded by long shadows and flickering candlelight, feet up and planning a break-in.

Our dinner had been brought to us by a friendly, chipmunkish kid about seven years old. He came in balancing two huge silver trays of food and said his name was Thomas of Uppington-on-Marsh. He talked nonstop while he lit the candles and laid out our meal, explaining that he was a page at Hampshire Castle and had been assigned to serve us while we were guests at the castle, but he would sleep on the kitchen floor as usual, so unless we had some other request, he would leave us now and get some rest, because tomorrow was going to be a big day because of Lady Elizabeth's birthday feast and everything.

I was all out of breath by the time he left, and I hadn't even said a word.

Max and I ate in silence, but I knew we were both thinking about the same thing—whether or not Flybender's time machine had broken down, leaving us stranded for good in the Middle Ages. When we finished eating, I leaned back, put my feet up on the chess table, and said, "So, Max, what do you think? We were only supposed to be here for eight hours, and it's been more than a day. What do you figure went wrong with the professor's fully guaranteed time machine?"

Max shook his head thoughtfully. "I don't know," he said slowly, "but I'm pretty sure it hasn't broken down completely. After all, it worked perfectly to begin with, and that proves the professor knew what he was doing. And a while ago I changed bodies, which at least shows that the time machine is doing *something*. That's a good sign."

"A good sign, *maybe*," I said doubtfully. "I mean, what's to keep you from shifting bodies again, only this time to a completely different time or a completely different place? We could be separated forever. You in ancient Egypt and me in medieval England—for the rest of our lives."

"I guess it could happen," said Max, nibbling on his thumbnail. He always does that when he's thinking hard. "But actually we have some pretty big problems right here, where we are. Like Sir Bevis, for instance. You're in real danger, Steve. Sir Bevis isn't going to forget about how you pushed him into the moat and beat him at the tournament. He'll try to get even with you, and I don't think he'll be too fussy about how."

We lapsed into silence.

"Got any ideas?" I said finally.

"Well, there is one possibility," said Max hesitantly. "I've been thinking about something Dr. Gathergoods said, something that caught my attention."

"The part about bat's blood and bits o' mummy?" I asked innocently.

Max glared at me. "No," he said, "the part about those ancient Arabian texts he has in his secret laboratory. Remember? He said they'd help him solve all kinds of mysteries, and that *even Time itself would do his bidding*."

Max paused. "So?" I said.

"So, let's suppose for a minute that Gathergoods really is on to something about time travel, and suppose the secret formula—or whatever it is—is lying around in those Arabian texts, just waiting for two brilliant guys like us to put it all together. We'd be home free!"

"Do you mean what I think you mean?" I said, snorting with disbelief. "Are you, the Man of Science, actually saying that some hocus-pocus recipe from some moldy old book could tell us how to travel through time? Now I've heard everything!"

"Look," Max protested, "I know it's a far-fetched idea, but right now it's our *only* idea. I think we should find a way to sneak into the doctor's secret laboratory, get our hands on those Arabian texts, and at least check them out. Don't forget, sometimes what people call magic is really just misunderstood science."

Motor-Mind had a point. It wasn't much of a plan, but what did we have to lose? At least we'd be *doing* something. Our only other choice was just to sit around and wait for Flybender's machine to wake up and work. And with Sir Bevis after me, I figured it was a good idea to try to get out of the Middle Ages while I was still alive.

"Okay," I said. "I'm game."

Now that we had a plan, we both felt a lot more relaxed. Max started humming to himself.

"I guess this means we have a busy day ahead of us tomorrow," he said cheerfully, "so I guess I'll hit the hay. Get it? Hit the *hay*!" He snickered. "Just a little hor—"

"I know, I know," I broke in, sighing. "Spare me."

A little horse humor goes a long way.

14

It's amazing how a little undercover work can brighten your day.

Max and I were up and eager first thing in the morning, plotting ways to get hold of Dr. Gathergoods's ancient Arabian texts. There was a short interruption when Thomas brought us our breakfast and filled us in on how the cooks had been up all night preparing special dishes for Lady Elizabeth's birthday feast, which was going to be the biggest one he'd ever seen, and even though the celebration didn't start until four o'clock, he had to go now and string flowers for garlands and change the reeds on the floor of the great hall because they were dirty and full of old bones, but he would see us later, good-bye.

Getting back to business, Max and I agreed that our main objective was to find Gathergoods's secret laboratory and to figure out how we were going to get in. I volunteered to case the castle, checking out the towers and other likely hideouts. Meanwhile, Max was going to talk to as many people as possible to see if he could pick up any helpful gossip or rumors. We agreed to meet back in our room and would have synchro-nized our watches if we had had any.

Within minutes, I was slinking across the court-yard and up a spiral staircase, heading for the top of the inner wall. Luckily, all the local people were scur-rying around, getting ready for the feast, so nobody paid any attention to me.

A few hours later, I was just about slinked out. I had explored all around the tops of both the inner and outer walls, peering into turrets, over battlements, down into gatehouses, and through narrow slit win-dows. All I had discovered were a few sleeping guards, a bunch of storerooms, and some great views of the surrounding countryside. No secret laboratory.

I decided to search the buildings that lined the walls of the inner bailey. I skirted the great hall, the kitchen, and the barracks, and sneaked into a large vine-covered building.

Figuring that a secret laboratory would be in a tower or at least somewhere up high, I decided to start at the top. I tiptoed up the stairs to the third floor. Ahead of me was a long, narrow corridor, with three doorways along one wall and several wall torches lean-ing out from the other. I peeked inside the first door and found I had stumbled onto someone's private liv-ing quarters. Judging from the huge canopied bed with velvet curtains, the fancy cushions on the chairs, and the gold dishes on the table, I guessed it was the apart-ment of someone very important, maybe even the Earl.

I swallowed hard. If I got caught snooping around here, I was going to have a very hard time explaining what I was doing. Somehow I didn't think the Earl would believe I was just out for an afternoon stroll—in his living room.

Retreat seemed like a good idea. So I took a deep breath, battened down my hatches, and took to my heels. The way I look at it, taking to your heels is always better than getting strung up by them.

But just as I reached the stairway, I heard voices coming from below. It was Dr. Gathergoods and the Hampshire Mauler, and they were headed my way!

I ran back down the hall and ducked into the same room. I might have dived under the bed, but as Gathergoods and Bevis stepped into the hall, I thought I heard my name. I left the door slightly open and listened.

"Sayest thou that his arrow did miss the target completely?" asked Sir Bevis as they passed by the door.

"Aye," replied the doctor, "and did strike the castle wall. 'Tis said 'twas a jest, but methinks the fall from his horse hath left Sir Robert a much-changed man."

"And a much-*weakened* man," said Sir Bevis with grim pleasure. "I must act before he regaineth his strength and skill." His voice began to fade down the hall. "This very day at the feast I shall . . ."

I strained to catch the rest, but it was no use. They were out of range. I shivered. I didn't know what Sir Bevis was planning to do at the feast—but I didn't think it was to ask if he could carve the turkey.

I was about to slip out and follow them when suddenly I felt a sharp tap-tap on my shoulder. I spun around. There, grinning up at me with her beady bird-eyes dancing, was old Agnes Longtooth.

"Agnes!" I sputtered. "What are *you* doing here?" A better question would have been what was *I* doing here?

"Why, I live here, in the adjoining room," she said. Then she added with a knowing wink, "But mayhap thou didst not know that this be Lady Elizabeth's private chamber." She snickered at the silliness of that thought.

I started to protest, but she held up her hand as a warning. "Hisst!" she whispered. "We must not be overheard." She scooted around me and closed the door.

I was trapped.

"Ah, Sir Robert," she said, whacking me playfully in the ribs, "truly thou art a lusty, brave youth to risk coming here. Lady Elizabeth will return within moments, but should the Earl find thee here, he would tear thee limb from limb."

Funny she should mention that. Being torn limb from limb just happens to be one of the two or three things I hate most. I decided to leave.

"In that case, Miss Longtooth," I said with what I hoped was a charming grin, "perhaps I'd better buzz off."

I grabbed for the door, but she backed firmly against it.

"Nay, nay, Sir Robert," she scolded, waggling her bony finger under my nose, "be not shy. Soon thy lady love will return and reward thy bravery with a kiss." She cackled happily, and then, placing her hand on her scrawny hip, she added thoughtfully, "Or perchance the Earl will arrive and throw thee out of yon window . . ."

I tried a feint to the left, hoping to draw her away from the door. No luck.

". . . as he did poor young Basil Fitzgerald when he did discover him here last year. Fortunately, the stout lad did grab the vine which groweth upon the wall, and began to climb down to the ground. He might have succeeded, too . . ."

This Agnes Longtooth should have been named Agnes Long*tongue*. How could I get her stopped?

". . . but alas, the Earl did seize the vine and shake it mightily. Poor Basil was thrown in an arc . . ."

Decking her with a right hook was definitely out.

". . . and did land among the pigs. He limped to his horse, pulled himself up, and rode away, groaning with great feeling." Agnes shifted her weight with a sort of flounce. "Or mayhap the Earl would kick thee down the stairs, as he did poor Henry Carmichael, who—"

"LOOK OUT FOR THE SPIDER!!!!!!!!" I yelled, pointing over Agnes's head.

With a shriek, she covered her head with her hands and lunged away from the door. I jerked it open and dived through.

Heh, heh, I chuckled to myself as I galloped down the hall to freedom. *The old look-out-for-the-spider trick gets 'em every time.*

15

Max was already back in our room when I burst through the door. He was on his knees, rummaging through one of Sir Robert's oak chests.

"I don't think you're going to find Dr. Gathergoods's laboratory in there," I said helpfully as I flopped into a chair and tried to catch my breath.

Max got up and stretched his legs. "I don't have to," he said, looking pleased with himself. "The fact is I already found out where the laboratory is."

I sat up straight. "Great! How'd you do it?"

"It was easy," he said, shrugging. "I just came right out and asked the blacksmith where Gathergoods's laboratory was, and he just came right out and told me. It's in the dungeon."

"The *dungeon*?" I said. I thought about all those hours I'd just spent sneaking around walls and towers. "Are you sure?"

"Positive," said Max. "The blacksmith says that about a year ago Gathergoods asked the Earl if he could have a tower, but the Earl said he wasn't going to give up a perfectly good tower for a bunch of crazy, crackpot experiments. He told Gathergoods that it was the dungeon—take it or leave it—and the doctor took it."

"But how can he use the dungeon?" I asked. "What about the prisoners?"

"There aren't any. It hasn't been used as a real dungeon for years."

"I still don't get it," I said. "If it's a *secret* laboratory, then how come this blacksmith guy knows where it is?"

"A good question," said Max, sort of snickering. "Are you ready for this? The blacksmith says *everyone* knows where it is, but nobody cares. And meanwhile, old Gathergoods spends half his time worrying about someone discovering his secret. He has a giant lock on the dungeon door, and he makes the blacksmith change it every week."

I frowned. "Do you think we'll be able to pick the lock?"

"We won't have to," said Max. "Because the blacksmith also says there's *another entrance to the dungeon*—an unlocked door hidden behind the unicorn tapestry in the great hall! Just about everyone in the castle knows it's there, but nobody's interested enough in Gathergoods's harebrained experiments to bother using it. *So,*" Max concluded with the satisfaction of a lawyer resting his case, "all we have to do is wait till the coast is clear in the great hall, sneak down into the dungeon, and help ourselves to those Arabian texts."

"And the sooner the better," I added, "because you were right, Max. Sir Bevis *is* planning to get even with me." I filled him in on the conversation I'd over-heard between Sir Bevis and Dr. Gathergoods.

Max looked worried. "There's no telling what Sir Bevis is up to," he said, "so I guess we'll just have to wait for him to make his move at the feast. In the meantime, you'd better carry this, just in case."

He reached into Sir Robert's trunk and took out a small dagger. On its gold scabbard was carved the head of a falcon, with two flashing emeralds for its eyes.

I took the dagger and tucked it inside my tunic.

"And keep an eye on Dr. Gathergoods, too," warned Max. "It looks like he just might be in cahoots with the Hampshire Mauler."

16

Max is what is known as a human bookhound. If there's a book anywhere within ten miles, he'll find it. So it's not surprising that by the time Thomas came to tell us the feast was on—come and get it—Max had already discovered a thin little book in Sir Robert's trunk and was slouched in a chair, happily reading away.

Meanwhile, I'd been saving my energy for some heavy-duty eating. As soon as Thomas left the room, I was on my feet, heading for the door.

"Come on," I said. "I'm starved!"

Max jumped up and blocked my way. "I can't let you do it!" he said. He had a look of deep, almost mournful, concern on his face and a suspicious twitch on his lips. "I just can't let you go out there and make a fool of yourself!"

I sighed. "What are you babbling about?"

"Steve," he said solemnly, "it has come to my attention that you are in need of a short, five-minute course in medieval manners before we go to the feast." He began to pace the floor. "After all, this is no school

79

lunchroom we're going to, you know. This is no crummy fast-food joint. This is a *formal banquet in the great hall of a great castle*! You and I, Steve, will be dining with refined ladies and well-bred gentlemen in an atmosphere of elegance and grace."

"So?" I said. "So I'll try not to spill my milk. Happy?"

Max shook his head sadly, as if I were a hopeless case, more to be pitied than blamed.

"If there is any hope for you at all," he said, "it is in this book." He briskly tapped the book he'd been reading, and then held it up so I could read the gold lettering on the cover: *The Booke of Gude Manners.*

"I found this wonderful little book in Sir Robert's trunk," he continued, "and it has all the latest on castle table manners. You don't want to look like a disgusting slob, do you? A vulgar oaf, a slovenly lout, an ill-mannered boor? An uncouth dullard, a rude and vile clod, a—"

"Okay, okay," I broke in. "You've got five minutes. But if I'm still a rude and vile clod after that, tough luck."

Max nodded and opened the little book with a dramatic flourish. He cleared his throat, peered at me over the top of the page, and began to read.

1. Use not the tablecloth as a nosecloth; nor within hearing of thy lord, trumpet thy nose loudly.
2. Butter not thy bread with thy thumb, nor dip too deeply thy hand into the sauce.
3. Neither shalt thou belch with a full mouth,

nor spit upon the floor or upon the walls.

4. The tossing of small bones to the dogs is quite correct and proper, but throw not a bone larger than thy foot.

Max skipped down to the bottom of the page. "And here's a couple of good ones to remember," he said.

9. If a morsel of food be not to thy liking, remove it from thy mouth with thy right hand alone. But wave it not for general inspection, nor make an unpleasant face at it.

10. Should a guest offend thee with a remark, strike him not, nor throw toward him any article of food.

Was he kidding? I grabbed the book and scanned the page. "Wipe not thy teeth upon the tablecloth," I read. He wasn't kidding.

I looked at Max. I could tell he was struggling to keep a straight face.

"Does this mean," I asked, "that I shouldn't turn the table over if I don't like the soup?"

"Not at all," replied Max, trying to sound prim but snickering instead. "Just be sure you fold your napkin first."

17

Max and I stepped out into the courtyard and joined the few stragglers who were hurrying toward the great hall. From inside came a wild confusion of music and laughter. The feast had begun.

We pushed through the huge carved door and stopped short, staring at the scene before us. In the center of the great hall, an enormous cavern of a room, a troupe of acrobats built a human pyramid almost up to the thick oak beams of the high ceiling, and then, on a signal, dissolved it in a tumble of spinning bodies. Minstrels strolled around the hall singing rowdy songs and sentimental ballads. Not far from us, the trained bear I had danced with at the fair was spinning slowly on his hind legs, stopping now and then to swipe at a pair of dogs that sniffed at him curiously.

Through a door in the wall to our left came a steady stream of servants carrying steaming platters of food over their heads. They had to dodge around the entertainers to serve the guests, who were sitting at long tables that lined three sides of the room. Against the fourth wall, in a black iron grate, a fire crackled beneath a deer roasting on a spit. All around the hall, the smoke from wall torches curled up to the ceiling.

Something on the far wall caught my eye, and I nudged Max. It was a huge tapestry. Even though it was faded with age, I could make out the scene—about a dozen hunters on horseback surrounding a forest, and in the middle of the forest, a white unicorn. Behind that tapestry was the secret door to the dungeon!

Max and I exchanged a meaningful glance.

Just then Thomas appeared and offered to show us to our seats, so we threaded our way to the table at the end of the room. I was surprised that Max was going to be sitting with me, since I was a knight and he was only a squire, but I guess the Earl wasn't too particular about rank.

The table was raised above the others on a platform, and sitting in the middle was the guest of honor, Lady Elizabeth. To her right were the Earl, Sir Bevis, and Dr. Gathergoods. To her left were two empty chairs, and at the end of the table, Agnes Longtooth.

Thomas ushered us up onto the platform and indicated that I should sit next to Lady Elizabeth. There was a brief scuffle as I tried to change places with Max but failed. A fine friend *he* was.

Agnes leaned around Max and called down the table to Lady Elizabeth, "I told thee he be shy!"

Lady Elizabeth giggled into her hand.

Max guffawed.

I blushed and got Max in the side with my elbow. Then I helped myself to a huge hunk of meat.

Everyone else dug in, too. And what a meal! The table was loaded with venison and duck and a whole roasted pig, and cheeses and fruits and huge loaves of bread, and cakes and pies and apples baked in honey—

with reinforcements arriving every few minutes.

The food was great, all right, but I'm sorry that I can't say the same for the manners of my fellow guests. In fact, it occurred to me that I should have brought along *The Booke of Gude Manners* and read it aloud to everyone there.

Even our host, the Earl, wasn't exactly a model of dignity and decorum. About halfway through the feast, I glanced over at him and saw that he was wiping his face—which was more or less covered with sauce—on the white tablecloth. When he finished, he cocked his head back and spat neatly across the table, narrowly missing a passing juggler.

Dr. Gathergoods got into the spirit of things by plunging his arm, almost up to his elbow, into a pot of stew. At first I thought he was stirring it. But after a lot of splashing around, he finally pulled out a huge onion, examined it closely with one eye as if it were the Hope Diamond, and then stuffed it into his mouth whole.

Sir Bevis was no Little Miss Goodmanners, either. With great energy, he slurped, smacked, gnawed, belched, and burped. He even gargled. He spilled things, he dropped things, he threw things. I think he would have *kicked* things if he could have gotten his feet up on the table.

I couldn't help wondering whether Lady Elizabeth was upset and embarrassed by everyone's terrible table manners, seeing as how it was her birthday party and she was the guest of honor. I sneaked a peek at her to see how she was handling it.

She caught my eye and smiled at me sweetly. Then she picked up a bone the size of a catcher's mitt and hurled it into the center of the hall. She had a good arm, too. Three dogs fell on the bone, snarling.

This gang, I thought to myself, would be a great help at one of our famous Camp Wongahana food fights.

In fact, I probably would have felt right at home if I hadn't been wondering the whole time what Sir Bevis had meant when he said he would make his move at the feast. Every few minutes I glanced down at him to be sure he was still in his seat and not sneaking up behind me with his evil-looking sword. Once I caught him staring at me while he was gnawing viciously at a bone. His eyes were glittering with hatred, and his greasy lips were curled into a sneer. He wiped his teeth on the tablecloth.

That was upsetting, all right, but it was small potatoes compared to another problem I had: Max and Agnes. From the very beginning of the feast, they had hit it off together just like two old army buddies who hadn't seen each other for forty years. They punched and poked each other; they cackled and guffawed and pounded the table; they laughed so hard they would have fallen out of their chairs if they hadn't had each other to hold on to. And what do you suppose was so hilarious? That's right. Me and Lady Elizabeth, of course.

Bits and pieces of their conversation drifted my way. For instance:

"Aren't they the cutest. . . . . . . ?"
And: ". . . adorable love birds . . . made for each other!"
And: "When . . . . wedding?"

Unfortunately, Lady Elizabeth overheard all this, too. Every time I peeked down the table at Sir Bevis, she thought I was making eyes at her. She went into a sort of permanent state of blush.

But the worst came during dessert, when suddenly a piercing cackle split the air.

"HEE, HEE, HEE!"

I peered around Max. Agnes was clutching his arm, with a huge, quivering grin on her face.

"Truly?" she crowed gleefully. "Did he truly say so?"

Max nodded vigorously. "Truly and verily, he *did*, he *did*!"

Agnes reached around behind Max and cuffed me on the back of the head. "Thou romantic devil!" she cried. Leaping spryly to her feet, she dashed by and began to whisper in Lady Elizabeth's ear.

I wondered whether it would be possible to drown myself in the stew.

All in all, it wasn't the most relaxing meal I'd ever had. So naturally I was relieved when the Earl decided to call it a night. He rose and thanked everyone for coming, wishing us all a good night.

Great, I thought. The feast was over, and Sir Bevis hadn't tried a single thing. He hadn't clubbed me with a bone or poisoned my punch. He hadn't even tried to steal my dessert. *Well*, I chuckled to myself as I started to get up, *that's the way it is with big-mouths. A lot of talk but no action. Talk, talk, talk, talk, t—*

"*Hold!*" cried Sir Bevis.

Everyone froze, halfway out of their chairs.

"M'lord," boomed Sir Bevis, addressing the Earl. "A great crime hath been committed!"

"What means this outburst?" demanded the Earl impatiently. " 'Tis my daughter's birthday and not a time for—"

Sir Bevis interrupted, trembling with rage. "I have such news as will not bear waiting, m'lord." His face blackened into a fierce scowl. Slowly, dramatically, he raised his arm and pointed his finger directly at me. Then, in a voice that echoed throughout the great hall, he thundered, "THAT MAN, WHO SHARETH THY TABLE AND ACCEPTETH THY HOSPITALITY, IS NAUGHT BUT A LOWLY THIEF!"

18

A shock wave surged through the great hall. The guests stared at each other in amazement and disbelief. *Sir Robert a thief?*

The Earl pounded the table with his fist. "Hast lost thy senses, Sir Bevis?" he demanded angrily. "Sir Robert is a knight of untainted reputation and is mine own true friend. Explain thyself. And thou best have good reason for this unseemly behavior!"

"I have reason enough and more, m'lord," answered Sir Bevis darkly, "for I do now accuse Sir Robert Marshall of *stealing Forkbeard's ear!*"

Once again, whispers of astonishment swept through the hall.

"Aye," continued Sir Bevis grimly. "As most of thee here know, my great-great-grandfather, Forkbeard, did lose his ear in battle some one hundred and fifty years ago. This ear hath become a treasured family heirloom and hath been kept these many years in the hollow pommel of the family sword. But, by'r Lady! Whilst Sir Robert did hold that sword for ransom on the final day of the tournament, he did discover the hollow compartment and did dishonorably steal my ancestor's ear."

The Hampshire Mauler turned and locked his eyes on mine. "And now, I demand my right to settle this affair in the manner provided by law—*a trial by combat*!"

The guests obviously didn't swallow Sir Bevis's story, and they began to grumble loudly against him. The Earl signaled for silence. He stroked his mustache for a few moments and then spoke.

"Sir Bevis, I will tell thee to thy face that I do not believe this vile accusation. Methinks thou hast brought this charge of theft against Sir Robert for selfish reasons. And yet, for all that, mayhap such a battle would resolve once and finally the rivalry between thee and Sir Robert." He looked down at me gravely. "What sayest thou, Green Falcon?"

"*If he refuseth to fight*," shouted Sir Bevis, "*he is a cringing coward*!"

"Nay, Sir Bevis," said the Earl, with a slight smile. "Sir Robert is not afeared to meet thee. In truth, what doth surprise me is that *thou*, who wert bested already at the tourney, art willing to cross swords with Sir Robert!"

From all around the hall there were murmurs of approval and even some scattered laughter. The Earl turned back to me.

"What sayest thou, Sir Robert?" he said. He sat down to wait for my reply.

I rose slowly to my feet and looked long and hard at Sir Bevis. Gradually, I allowed the corner of my mouth to turn down into a contemptuous sneer. I remembered the dagger Max had given me, so I drew it out of my tunic and began to pick my teeth with it.

Finally, I spoke—evenly, scornfully, with my eyes narrowed dangerously.

"Coward? Me, a coward? *Don't make me laugh!*" I gave a brief, harsh laugh. "I am Sir Robert Marshall, the Green Falcon. I fear no man! I fear no mauler!"

I looked at Sir Bevis as if he were a worm. Then I ran my finger back and forth along the blade of the dagger.

"Sir Bevis," I continued, "thou knowest full well that I have never laid a hand on thy great-great-grandfather's ear. But if thou art determined to fight, then name thy time and place, and we will settle this matter once and for all!"

The Hampshire Mauler smirked triumphantly. "On the morrow then, at one o'clock in the outer bailey, where there is room for a man to wield a sword freely."

"Done!" I agreed.

Then, with the coiled control of a gunfighter walking the dangerous streets of a western town, I pushed back my chair and strode slowly, coolly, across the great hall. Max scurried around in front of me and opened the huge door so I wouldn't have to break my stride.

The guests watched my exit in silent awe and admiration.

As soon as Max had pushed the door closed behind us, I staggered weakly over to the wall and crumpled against it for support. *"I'm a goner!"* I squeaked. *"Done for. Finished."*

Max chewed his thumbnail thoughtfully for a minute and then, in a no-nonsense voice, said, "Looks like we'll have to sneak down into Gathergoods's secret lab tonight. But if we don't find any information on time travel there, I think we should saddle up the horses and make a run for it before morning."

Good old practical Max. I mean, this wasn't the most brilliant plan I'd ever heard, but I was in no mood to be picky.

"Right," I said, testing my knees to see if they'd hold my weight.

19

Hours later, Max and I were standing in a pale pool of torchlight in the dark, deserted great hall. Max pushed back the heavy unicorn tapestry and uncovered a thick wooden door with rusty hinges. A distant bell tolled as I grasped the iron latch ring with both hands and pulled, straining against the weight and rust. Sloooo-oooowly, with a rasping groan that echoed through the hall, the door swung open.

A cold wind, smelling musty and tomblike, struck our faces. The light from our flickering torch pierced the blackness for a few feet only, revealing a narrow stone passageway that sloped sharply downward. The walls and floor were wet and glistening, and from somewhere below came a hollow dripping sound, like a warning. Three hairy, black, egg-sized spiders backed away into the darkness.

"After you," I said.

Max squinted into the tunnel. "Age before beauty," he said, not budging.

"Squire before knight," I countered, wondering if the spiders were lying in ambush up ahead.

"Tall before short," said Max, shoving the torch into my hand.

I sighed. *Somebody* had to go first. So, holding the torch ahead of me with one hand and groping along the cold, wet wall with the other, I started into the tunnel. It led downward for thirty or forty feet, twisted to the left, and then dropped even more steeply. As I rounded a corner, my foot slipped on the wet stones and I fell. My hand came down on something squishy.

When Max leaned down to help me up, a small black shape skittered across his arm. He yelped, and I jumped up, brushing my head against the sticky webs that hung from the low ceiling. Something with a lot of legs galloped down my back.

I didn't try to find out what it was. I batted at it with my hand, and it landed with a THUNK on the wet floor. Grabbing Max's arm, I pulled him on down the tunnel. "Let's get going," I said, shivering.

The tunnel seemed endless. Downward and downward it went, but finally we saw the dim outlines of a door ahead. Quietly, we crept down to it, pressed our ears against the damp wood, and listened. There were no voices. The coast was clear. Together we pushed the door open and stepped into a large low-ceilinged room.

Jackpot! It was Dr. Gathergoods's secret laboratory, all right. Huge vats of slimy green brew were bubbling over fires, filling the room with clouds of eerie green steam. Strings of dried bats and toads hung from the walls. A long, tilting table was piled high with moldy books, and all around the room were shelves cluttered with multicolored bottles and vials. There was even some sort of Egyptian mummy, with loose gray wrappings, propped against a lionskin chair. In the far corner of the lab was a pile of shattered glass and mangled metal—the remains, I guessed, of a recent explosion.

It reminded me of my room back home, and a wave of homesickness passed over me. I half-expected my mother to come bursting in, demanding to know just when I intended to clean up this mess.

But there was no time for fond memories now. There were dozens of lighted candles all around the laboratory, so I figured Dr. Gathergoods had to be somewhere nearby. I posted myself near the main entrance as a lookout, while Max made a beeline for the books. He quickly leafed through one that was lying open on the table, shook his head, and then checked out several others.

"So?" I asked in a loud whisper. "Found anything on time travel yet?"

"Not exactly," said Max, snapping the last book shut. "I regret to say that when we mapped out this wonderful plan, we overlooked one small problem."

He tapped the books with his fingertip. "We overlooked the fact that these ancient Arabian texts are written in *Arabic*!"

It took a few seconds for that bit of news to sink in. When it did, I gaped at Max and blurted, "You mean we *can't even read them*? Of all the stupid—"

But before I could finish, I caught the sound of voices approaching the main entrance.

"Take cover!" I hissed. "Somebody's coming!"

Max ducked under the table and pulled a stuffed

owl and a stack of books in front of him. I wedged myself behind an empty cauldron.

Dr. Gathergoods swept into his secret lab.

"I will not!" he was protesting loudly. Clouds of green vapor swirled around his head. " 'Tis true I did spy on Sir Robert for thee, for thou didst promise me supplies unlimited for my experiments. But thou hast gone too far this time, Sir Bevis!"

Sir Bevis strode into the lab on the doctor's heels. "Thou wilt do as thou art told," he growled angrily, "or . . ."

He ripped a dried toad off the wall and crushed it viciously in one hand. Then he held the crumbled remains under Gathergoods's nose and let the dust fall slowly to the floor.

I had to hand it to him. Sir Bevis knew how to make a point.

Dr. Gathergoods let out a faint squeak. "But," he argued weakly, "thou art taking unfair advantage of Sir Robert, who thou knowest is not himself. And . . . and . . . the *Earl*!"

"Aye," snarled Sir Bevis, "the Earl. Thou didst hear how he did take Sir Robert's part against me at the feast. For that, he will die!"

Dr. Gathergoods moaned, wringing his hands.

"On the morrow," continued Sir Bevis with evil relish, "I will slay that arrogant fool, Sir Robert. And then I will marry Lady Elizabeth, making myself heir to Hampshire fiefdom. And finally, my dear doctor, the high and mighty Earl will be dispatched, suddenly and mysteriously. And thou wilt provide me with a poison to do the deed!"

"No!" gasped the doctor, backing away.

"Or I will boil thee in one of thine own vile brews and use the result as the poison I need!" Sir Bevis laughed nastily at his joke.

Dr. Gathergoods shut his eyes in horror and then, suddenly, he made a dash for the door and disappeared up the passageway. Sir Bevis followed him, his crude laughter echoing through the stone corridor.

After several minutes of tense silence, Max and I rose slowly from our hiding places and exchanged somber looks. Making a run for it was out of the question now. We both understood that. We couldn't just leave the Earl and Lady Elizabeth at the mercy of the Hampshire Mauler.

Sir Bevis had to be stopped, and it was up to me to do it.

I just hoped he'd be willing to give up his trial-by-combat idea and have a spelling bee instead.

20

The next morning Thomas brought us a late breakfast and a castle-news update. Everyone, he said happily, was in high spirits, looking forward to the battle and laying heavy odds in my favor, although there were a few who thought that Sir Bevis had a chance, but that was silly because everyone knew that those with justice and fair play on their side always won these trials by combat, and anyway, he'd see us later. He had to go help build a platform for the Earl and Lady Elizabeth to view the trial from.

Max pushed a sausage around on his plate. "Maybe we should just go to the Earl and tell him about Sir Bevis's plot," he said.

"We have no proof," I pointed out. "It'd just look like I was trying to worm out of the fight."

"I guess you're right," he sighed. He frowned to himself for a while and then added hopefully, "Maybe I could fix you up with a written excuse from home."

"I don't think so," I said, helping myself to some eggs.

Max lapsed into a gloomy silence.

It was nice to know he was concerned about me, but actually I wasn't all that worried myself. I'd been thinking the whole thing over, and I'd decided I wasn't really in any danger. In fact, I was feeling pretty good.

"Cheer up," I said. "You seem to have forgotten a very important fact. Mainly, that I've got all of Sir Robert's amazing talent right at my fingertips."

"How do you figure that?" said Max.

"Simple. Isn't this Sir Robert's body I'm wearing? And isn't he an expert swordsman? Well, let's face it. That makes *me* an expert swordsman. You see that arm?" I held out my arm. "It's probably made more thrusts and parries than you could count. I mean, sword fighting is second nature to this arm."

Max's eyes lit up, and I could almost see his Motor-Mind shifting into high gear.

"You may just have something there, Steve," he said eagerly. "Hmmmmm, yes . . . second nature . . . I can definitely see some possibilities there."

He jumped to his feet and began to pace around the room with his hands folded behind his back. "I could call it the Theory of Patterned-Reflex Response. Through long years of training, the body has been conditioned to respond to specific actions with specific reactions. These responses are now completely automatic and, like breathing, they require no thought."

Max stopped abruptly and looked down at me. "No use wasting time. Let's test the theory right now."

Well, I thought, *why not*? I was sort of interested in seeing how it felt to be the best swordsman in England. I wolfed down the last of my breakfast and then got Sir Robert's sword and buckled it around my waist.

"Okay," said Max. "Let's say that candelabra is Sir Bevis." He pointed to the silver candelabra in the middle of the table. It had five tall candles in it. "For your first test, how about if you whip out your sword and whack those candles in two."

I shook my head. "Too easy."

Max raised his eyebrows. "Oh? And what did you have in mind, Captain Marvel?"

"Something a little more challenging," I said, cracking my knuckles. "For instance, see that apple? Take it and stand over there on the other side of the room. When you give the signal, I'll go for my sword and you toss the apple toward me at the same time. Before it gets here, I'll make two clean slices through all five candles, and then I'll run the apple through in midair."

"A feat worthy of Sir Robert," agreed Max, heading for the far side of the room with the apple.

I positioned myself in front of the candelabra in a sturdy, spread-foot stance, my hands resting on my hips.

"Ready?" he said.

"Are you kidding? The Green Falcon is always ready."

"*Draw!*" he shouted, and at the same moment, he lobbed the apple in my direction.

With lightning speed, I went for my sword.

A lot of things happened at once.

I jerked the sword out of the scabbard.

It flew out of my hand.

Max took cover behind a leather chair.

The apple caught me in the mouth.

And the sword sailed smoothly—gracefully— across the room and stuck with a loud *twannnggg!* into the high back of the leather chair.

Max peered cautiously around the side of the chair. "So much for the Theory of Patterned-Reflex Response," he muttered.

"Well, look at it this way," I said. "If there's a choice of weapons, I can always ask for a harpoon."

21

I don't like to brag, but the fact is I'm not the kind of guy a person should mess with. Push me a little too far, and you've got trouble. Big trouble. And I proved exactly that as I practiced my swordsmanship the rest of the morning. I don't think I'd be tooting my own horn too much if I said that within a few hours' time I had made mincemeat of those five candles.

And I won't even mention the poor apple.

Meanwhile, Max and I had also come up with a clever plot of our own to counter Sir Bevis's evil scheme, and Max had disappeared for a while to lay the groundwork. When he came back, he was grinning happily.

"It's all set," he said. "I talked to Dr. Gathergoods like we planned. I sort of cornered him in the courtyard and told him we knew all about Sir Bevis's rotten plot. I said it was a pretty dirty trick to take advantage of you when he knew perfectly well you had a head injury from falling off your horse and were in no condition to fight. Old Gathergoods was so upset he almost cried. He said he most humbly begged your pardon for his part in the plot, and that he would gladly help us if only he knew how. So . . . I told him how."

"And he said he'd do it?"

"Yep. Just before the trial, he'll slip a pinch of one of his potions into Sir Bevis's wine. So by the time you cross swords with the Hampshire Mauler, he'll be so wobbly and woozy he'll wish that he'd never gotten out of bed this morning. You'll be able to knock him over with a feather."

We chuckled wickedly at the beauty of it all.

"Of course," Max added, "I had to promise you wouldn't hurt Sir Bevis while he's in a weakened state."

"Of course," I agreed. "By the way, what's good old Gathergoods going to spike Sir Bevis's drink with?"

"I didn't have the stomach to ask, but I thought I heard him mumble something about oil of snake and dried crocodile dung."

We were still guffawing when Thomas knocked on the door and announced that it was time for the trial to begin.

We sallied forth in high spirits. I was wearing my chain-mail armor, green tunic, and sword. Max was carrying my helmet and shield. As we passed through the archway and into the outer bailey, a welcoming shout went up from the spectators. There were hundreds of them, all crowded into the courtyard and along the tops of the walls.

Max and I made the rounds, shaking hands and kidding with the crowd. I bowed deeply to Lady Elizabeth and jokingly asked Agnes if she'd seen any spiders lately. Agnes dissolved into cackles, and Lady Elizabeth gave me a gold chain to wear "for good luck." The crowd roared with laughter when I paused beside two squires holding a stretcher and called across the courtyard, "Hey, Sir Bevis, here's your stretcher! I hope it fits!"

Sir Bevis snarled, baring his teeth.

Then, while the Earl made a speech about "the good name of Justice and those who would sully it," Sir Bevis and Dr. Gathergoods shared a quick toast. They said something we couldn't hear, clinked their goblets together, and drank down their wine. Then Gathergoods tossed his hair out of his eyes and winked across the courtyard at us. That was the signal that the deed was done. Sir Bevis had drunk the potion.

Max leaned over, handed me my helmet and shield, and whispered, "Remember to take it easy on Sir Bevis. In a few seconds the poor guy is going to be sick as a dog." He snickered. "Or maybe a crocodile."

I struggled to keep a straight face as the Earl ended his speech with a lordly, "*Let the combat begin!*"

Suddenly, the spectators grew tense and quiet. They drew back from the center of the courtyard, leaving me face to face with the Hampshire Mauler.

The potion was working! No doubt about it, Sir Bevis was *definitely* not well. He was already beginning to sway on his feet, and there was a glassy look in his eyes. Even his evil sneer seemed ragged around the edges.

Heh, heh, I chuckled to myself. This mauler couldn't maul his way out of a paper bag. I just hoped

I'd have time to get in some fancy footwork, a bit of razzle-dazzle swordplay, and maybe a few flying leaps before Sir Bevis fell flat on his face.

To speed things up, I quickly slipped on my helmet and, with a flourish, drew out my sword. It made a satisfying sssssssst sound. I stood ready.

Sir Bevis gripped his sword and drew it out. SSSSSSSSSSSSSSSSSSTTT!!!!

I didn't like the sound of that.

And I didn't much care for the way he began to limber up, making about a dozen lightning-fast slashes through the air with his sword: SWAAP! SWAAP! SWAAP! SWAAP! SWAAP! SWAAP! SWAAP! SWAAP! SWAAP! SWAAP! SWAAP! SWAAP!

I mean, shouldn't he have been just sort of standing there limply, staring at his sword and trying to figure out what it was doing in his hand?

I glanced over at Dr. Gathergoods, and I was not very happy about what I saw.

Dr. Gathergoods was looking wobbly and woozy and green around the gills. He clutched his stomach and reeled to the right. He rolled his eyes and stumbled to the left. He staggered around in a circle and then pitched over backward, falling up, over, and behind a horse trough. Only his feet stuck up over the top. They waggled weakly.

I felt a bit waggly and weak myself as I realized that goofy Gathergoods had gotten his goblets mixed up and had swallowed the potion himself.

Which explained why Sir Bevis was looking so healthy. He *was* healthy. What I had thought was a sway was a swagger. That glassiness had been a glint.

The Hampshire Mauler began circling me slowly,

closing in, crouching slightly. His sword gleamed in the sun.

Things looked very, very poor in the Staying-Alive Department.

I broke into a cold sweat and began backing away. What I needed now was a brand-new, extremely clever plan. Or maybe just an ordinary, everyday miracle. I shot a quick glance at Max, but he wasn't any help. He was just standing there, staring at Dr. Gathergoods's feet with a stunned expression on his face.

Sir Bevis gave a low, fiendish, gloating laugh. He smelled victory and was loving it. "Now, varlet," he jeered, "I will send thee to thy doom!"

I wasn't about to let him know I was scared.

"You and who else, pipsqueak?" I said, still backing away.

I was about to add that his mother wore army boots, but there wasn't time. Because suddenly, I was upside down.

Upside down? What was I doing upside down? Sir Bevis hadn't even swung at me!

I looked around wildly. There *was* no Sir Bevis! And no castle! No Max, no Gathergoods, no Lady Elizabeth, no Agnes, no Earl! Nothing but a whirl of flashing, streaking lights and a wind that blew and blustered and moaned like a hurricane.

I landed with a crash.

On the old, rumpled cot in our clubhouse. In front of me—wheezing, grumbling, rattling, and spewing steam—was Professor Flybender's Fully Guaranteed One-Of-A-Kind Time Machine.

It looked worn out. It gasped. It burped.

I was home.

22

A few seconds later, Max appeared.

Or rather a large, fuzzy, Max-like *shape* appeared—high up near the ceiling of the clubhouse. The time machine seemed to be having trouble tuning him in. It sputtered and coughed and seemed to give up. Then it revved up with a whine and tried again. Meters went wild. The clubhouse shook. A window cracked.

And then, suddenly, the fuzzy shape came into focus.

It was Max all right, stretched out flat against the ceiling, looking down. An expression of wild-eyed alarm spread over his face as he considered his situation. Flybender's machine sighed and turned itself off.

With a loud "aaaaaaaaaAAAAAAAA!!!" Max plummeted to the floor.

I rushed over and helped him to his feet. "You okay?" I asked.

"It's nothing," he muttered, checking himself over for injuries. "What's a little thing like a broken body?" He glared at the time machine with disgust. "But if we ever use that crazy contraption again, I'm going to wear a parachute and a crash helmet."

I laughed. "Well, what'd you expect from a time machine that can't even tell time and got us back three days late. Did you think it'd bring you back all nice and snug and tucked in bed?"

"Maybe not," said Max, limping around in a circle, "but it would have been nice."

He stopped short. "Three days . . . hmmmm, yes . . . that would explain it." Max went over to the time machine, pushed his glasses back up on his nose, and peered at the control panel. "Ah-ha! Just as I suspected. There wasn't any problem with the machine at all! The problem, fumble fingers, was *you*. When you thought you were changing our Length-of-Stay from three hours to eight hours, you turned the wrong knob. See? The numbers control is still on 003. You turned the *units* knob by mistake—so it went from hours to days to years to minutes to hours and ended up on days. That left the control reading '003 *days*,' which is exactly how long we were gone."

I squinted at the control panel and then straightened up and grinned at Max.

"Do you realize what this means?" I said. "It means this thing works just like it's supposed to, and we could use it again any time we want." I gave the time machine a friendly pat. "Good old Professor Flybender. He really knew his stuff."

"Yeah," said Max, polishing his glasses on his shirt tail. "Even that business of my being unstable in the Middle Ages wasn't the time machine's fault. It was just that I had one foot out the door when you started the machine, and it was never able to focus on me properly. That's why I changed bodies and all. And that's why I stayed in the Middle Ages longer than you did, too. If it hadn't been for—"

"Hey, wait a minute," I interrupted. "What do you mean you stayed in the Middle Ages longer than I did? Didn't we leave at the same time?"

"No," said Max matter-of-factly. "I was there about fifteen minutes longer than you. I guess the time machine just had to work harder to get hold of me. Of course, we arrived back here at the same time because that's the way the machine works. Remember? No matter how long you're gone, you arrive back exactly when you left."

I stared at him. "Do you mean to tell me you know what happened after I left Hampshire Castle? How the battle came out and everything, and *you haven't told me yet*!"

"Sure," said Max. "I saw the whole thing."

"Well?" I demanded. *"What happened?"*

Max shrugged his shoulders and tried to look bored. "It was nothing. Just a lot of swordfighting, a lot of kissing, a lot of fainting, and a lot of splashing around in the horse trough. You wouldn't be interested."

He tied his shoelaces.

"MAX!" I threatened.

"Okay, okay," he said, grinning. "But listen closely, because I'm a very busy guy, and I don't want to have to repeat myself."

"Will you get on with it?" I said.

Max tapped his chin thoughtfully. "Well, let's see.

Right after you left the Middle Ages, Sir—"

"Hold it," I said. "How'd you know when I left?"

"Because I saw your body quivering, and I recognized the symptoms. That's how. Anyway, right after you left, Sir Robert took over his own body again and for a minute I thought he was going to keel right over. He looked all dizzy and confused and he didn't even seem to notice Sir Bevis closing in on him. It looked like it was all over for Sir Robert. But at the last minute, he sort of shook himself hard, raised his sword, and charged Sir Bevis. And then, wow! What a swordfight! It was great!"

Max began to battle his way around the time machine, slashing the air with an imaginary sword.

"Did Sir Robert make any flying leaps?" I asked hopefully.

"No, but he was terrific. He made Sir Bevis look like a two-year-old. He just backed him up step by step until suddenly he knocked the sword right out of Sir Bevis's hand. Boy, was Sir Bevis scared. There he was, with his back to the wall and Sir Robert's sword at his throat. There wasn't a sound in the whole courtyard. Everyone was waiting for Sir Robert to run him through."

Max paused, remembering the scene.

"Well?" I said. "Did he?"

"Are you kidding?" scoffed Max. "Not the Green Falcon. He's too noble for that. He lowered his sword and said, 'This fight is not of my making,' and then he let the Earl decide what to do with Sir Bevis.

"So the Earl told Sir Bevis never to darken his drawbridge again and banished him from the fiefdom.

And that was it for Sir Bevis. He just sort of slunk away, muttering to himself and glaring at anyone who got in his way. He tried to kick a chicken, but it pecked him."

Max and I snickered.

"After that," Max went on, "Lady Elizabeth more or less threw herself into Sir Robert's arms, and he didn't throw her out again. In fact, he kissed her. More than once."

I was amazed. "And the Earl didn't tear him limb from limb?"

"No, the Earl looked pretty pleased about the whole thing. *Everybody* looked pleased. Especially old Agnes Longtooth. She was so overcome with joy that she fainted dead away and fell right into Dr. Gathergoods's arms. And he—"

"Dr. Gathergoods?" I broke in. "The last time I saw him, he was lying behind the horse trough with both feet in the air."

"Yeah, but he'd managed to drag himself to his feet and was sort of staggering out to the center of the bailey when Agnes collapsed on him. I don't think he even recognized her. He just lifted her up in his arms and stared down at her, kind of puzzled. I think he was trying to figure out why her tongue was hanging out. Anyway, all of a sudden, his eyes shot wide open and he yelled, ' 'Tis a damsel in distress!' He held her up for everyone to see and then he said, 'Never fear, fair lady. Thou art in the capable hands of Dr. Clarence Gathergoods!' "

"Poor Agnes," I said, chuckling.

"Poor Agnes is right," said Max, "because then Gathergoods lost his balance and started stumbling

110

backward. He tripped over his robe, spun around, and dropped Agnes right into the horse trough. And the last thing I saw in the Middle Ages was Agnes splashing angrily around in the water and good old Gathergoods waving his arms and yelling, 'Fetch my bag! There is a lady in the horse trough!' "

Max and I cracked up and laughed for a couple of minutes straight. Then I asked him to tell me about the battle all over again. While he was talking, I got to thinking about all the fun I'd had being Sir Robert—winning the tournament and going on the hunt and dancing with the bear and booting Sir Bevis into the moat and everything. I felt a little sad. When Max finished, I gave a long sigh.

"You know, Max," I said, "it was kind of nice being a legend in my own time."

I thought about it some more. Then I sighed again.

"And you know what?" I went on. "I really do think that Sir Robert and I had a lot in common. You know, strength of character, quick wit, fearlessness in the face of danger. Things like that."

I cracked my knuckles.

Max gave something close to a horse snort. "Oh, sure," he said, "and let's not forget your famous ability to woo the ladies." He snickered noisily. "I mean, you should have *seen* yourself at the feast, sitting next to Lady Elizabeth. Wow! You looked so embarrassed that Agnes and I thought you were going to try to slide down under the table and crawl away!"

Max almost choked, he thought that was so funny. I glared at him.

"Was your face *red*!" he gasped. "If I hadn't

known it was you, I'd have thought there was a big beet sitting in your chair!" He gave a gleeful hoot. *"A big red beet wearing a tunic!"*

Max dissolved into gales of laughter, sort of staggering around the clubhouse for a while and then collapsing against the time machine and sliding down onto the floor. He cackled and snorted and pounded the floor with his hands.

I pretended to ignore him. With great dignity, I cleared a place for myself at the table, sat down, picked up a pencil and a clean sheet of paper, and began composing a letter.

After several disgusting minutes, Max's laughter died down to the hiccup-and-sigh stage. He rolled over and looked up at me.

"What're you doing?" he asked with an exhausted chuckle. "Counting the precious hours you and Lady Elizabeth spent together?" He managed a weak snickering fit of five or six snickers. I waited for him to recover.

Then I looked him straight in the eye with an expression of true-blue sincerity and noble self-sacrifice. "No, Max. What I'm doing is saving you a lot of time, trouble, and hard work. It's the least I can do, considering everything you did for me while we were in the Middle Ages."

Max struggled to his feet, suddenly suspicious. "What do you mean?" he asked. He edged closer to the table and tried to peek at my paper. I held it away.

"I mean, Max, old buddy, that I've just done you a big favor. I've just written your second letter to Dawn Sharington for you. And I think I can say that this letter will live in her memory forever. And it'll be a big hit at the slumber party she's giving for all her friends next weekend."

Max started to protest, but I held up my hand. "Wait!" I said, smiling modestly. "Don't thank me yet. You should hear the letter first. How's this for an eye-catching opening?

MY DARLING DAWN!
   HOW MY HEART DOTH YEARN FOR THEE!"

Max's mouth dropped open.
"It gets better," I said enthusiastically. "Listen to this:

I AM THY DEVOTED SLAVE FOR LIFE, MY
LOVE. DO WITH ME WHAT THOU WILT."

Max choked and his eyes bugged out. He looked as if he had just swallowed a slimy green toad.
"And get this. She'll *love* this part:

MY LIFE IS A TORMENT WITHOUT THEE, DAWN,
DEAREST! WILT THOU BE MINE?

"And I'm signing it,

YOUR EVER-LOVING MAX."

I grinned evilly. "Well, what do you think, lover boy?"

Max gnashed his teeth, let out a roar, and lunged

for me. I dodged around the time machine and high-tailed it out of the clubhouse—with the letter in my hand and Max hot on my heels.

It was a great feeling to be home again and back in the old routine.